I0570810

Waking Dreams

A Soul's Mark Novella

ASHLEY STOYANOFF

Copyright © 2013 Ashley Stoyanoff
ISBN: 0988077590
ISBN-13: 978-0988077591

ALL RIGHTS RESERVED. This book contains material
protected under International and Federal Copyright Laws
and Treaties. Any unauthorized reprint or use of this
material is prohibited. No part of this book may be
reproduced or transmitted in any form or by any means,
electronic or mechanical, including photocopying, recording,
or by any information storage and retrieval system without
express written permission from the author / publisher.

Published by Ashley Stoyanoff Books
www.ashleystoyanoff.com

Edited by Kathryn Calvert

Cover design by ebookindiecovers.com

This is a work of fiction. Names, characters, places, and
incidents are the products of the author's imagination or are
used fictitiously. Any resemblance to actual events, locales,
or persons, living or dead, is entirely coincidental.

ACKNOWLEDGMENTS

To my sister Jonel, I couldn't have finished this without all of your support and encouragement—thank you. A special thanks to my mother Jo-Anne—your feedback and honesty kept me going when I wanted to give up. Further thanks to my editor Kathryn. Without your technical expertise and assistance, this book would not have been finished. Most of all, I would like to thank my husband Jordan, whose unwavering patience and support has made it possible for me to finish Waking Dreams.

BOOKS BY ASHLEY STOYANOFF

The Soul's Mark Series
The Soul's Mark: FOUND
Waking Dreams, A Soul's Mark Novella
The Soul's Mark: HUNTED
The Soul's Mark: BROKEN
The Soul's Mark: CHANGED

Deadly Trilogy
Deadly Crush

CHAPTER 1

Sterling snorted, and her left ear twitched to the side. "What do you hear, girl?" Eric asked, stroking his mare's thick neck. His teeth chattered, and his breath puffed out in a cloud of white fog. She jumped to the right, and pawed at the snowy ground, with jittery, nervous strikes. Her ears pinned flat against her neck, and she glared at the tree line.

Eric searched the ice-encrusted trees for what may have spooked his horse, but he saw nothing. Creaks and cracks from the trees drifted to his ears, as the branches sagged under the weight of the ice, but aside from that, the forest was silent and still. He stroked her mane and cooed calming words to her, and after a moment, she began to settle.

Giving her a gentle nudge, he reined Sterling back to the fence. A gust of frosty wind blew through the field, and a shiver prickled over his skin. It had been a long day, rounding up the cattle that had gotten loose during the ice storm last night. Now, if he could just find the broken place in the fence and mend it, he would finally be able to get back into the warmth of his ranch house.

Sterling walked along the rails slowly, picking her footing with care. The sun shone brightly, winking upon the icy ground and making the field look like a sea of glittering gems. Breathtaking. It was sights like this that reminded Eric why he had chosen to live so far from the village, on his own, surrounded by nature. His mother had called him a fool, not understanding why anyone would choose to farm and live an hour's ride from civilization if they did not have to. But to Eric, the peace and wilderness was like living a dream.

After a good twenty minutes, he finally stumbled upon the broken rails which were buried beneath a crusty layer of snow and ice. Eric slid off of Sterling's back, and gave her a pat as he unhitched the fencing wire from the saddle, and then he got to work, breaking off the crunchy layers of snow, and yanking out the snapped rails.

Once the three broken rails were down, Eric dug through the snow for the spares, which he knew were resting just below, against the fence. He had just pulled the first rail free, when he heard Sterling snort and squeal.

"Settle down, girl," he said. He dropped the rail in place and turned, pacing towards her. Her eyes were wild—panicked—and her nostrils flared. He put his hands up and he crouched, slumping his shoulders, trying to make his bulky frame smaller and less intimidating. The last thing he needed was for her to bolt, and leave him to walk back to the house in this frigid weather. "Easy girl," he murmured, as he continued towards her.

Sterling pranced around nervously, watching him with frightened eyes. She snorted and began to back up with her ears lying flat against her neck. Eric reached out for a rein, slowly, carefully, and just as his hand closed around it, she let out a piercing high-pitched roar, and then she reared.

Too close, a voice in his head shouted, and he scrambled back. His foot caught a patch of ice and slid out from under him, and he landed on his back with a jarring thud, sliding closer to her and cracking his head against frozen ground. Her hooves came down fast and hard, so close to him, that he was certain she would come down right on him. He tried to roll out of the way, but he couldn't move quickly enough.

And in a blink, she was on him, her hoof came down on his stomach, and then it jumped across and skidded down his right side, ripping at his skin and muscles. She roared again, drowning out Eric's wheezing cry. For a spilt-second, she looked down at him; her eyes were wide with fear, and then she bolted, racing away through the field.

Eric couldn't breathe. He couldn't move. Black spots danced through his vision, and a stabbing pain shot through his head all the way down to his toes. A warm wetness spread along the base of his skull, and his stomach convulsed with pain.

Time stood still. His ears rung, and he couldn't catch his breath. He tried to sit up, but he couldn't. Even the slightest movement sent hot waves of pain coursing through his body, paralyzing him. *Get up! You need to get up!* he told himself over and over, trying to coax his body to ignore the shooting pain and begging his mind to fight for survival. But no matter how much his brain wanted to survive, his body was shutting down—giving up.

Eric didn't know how long he had been lying on the ground, fighting against his body. It could have been seconds, or it might have been hours when he heard the crunch of snow nearby. It was excruciatingly loud, and the sound sent shockwaves through his head. A small sense of hope gripped at his chest. He forced in a burning breath, and opened his mouth to yell for help just as a shadow fell over him. He blinked and shifted his gaze, looking for the source of the shadow, and he found it, but in that moment, all he noticed was the pair of blazing red eyes staring down at him.

"Demon," Eric breathed and gasped, a wet and painful sound, and he coughed, choking on his own saliva. He tried to scramble away, but the pain ceased him, rendering the effort useless. The demon smiled, which might have been meant as a friendly gesture, but the dagger sharp fangs that protruded from his mouth were anything but welcoming.

"What's your name, son?" the demon asked, folding his

3

arms over his thick chest. His voice was like velvet, alluring and comforting. Eric froze and looked back at him, mesmerized by the sound. The demon was tall, at least four inches taller than Eric's own six feet, and he had the same muscular frame. He had no jacket or gloves, only wearing a thin short sleeve shirt and woven cotton slacks. His skin was flawless, the color of ivory.

He chuckled, and his blazing eyes danced with amusement. "Your name?" he repeated, and his smile grew.

Eric opened his mouth to speak, but the words were lodged in his throat. He cleared it, and his voice shook as he answered, "Eric Carter."

The demon watched him with a thoughtful expression for a moment, and his crimson eyes faded to sky-blue. He bent down, crouching beside Eric in the snow. He reached out, ripped open Eric's coat, and lifted his shirt. Blood pooled below his skin where Sterling had landed, blackening his stomach.

"Well, Mr. Carter, it looks like you are about to die," he said with a matter-of-fact tone, as if it was common knowledge, obvious even.

"Yes, sir," Eric replied breathlessly, wincing as the demon poked at his stomach. For a moment, he wondered why he was not trying to run, but then he looked back at the angelic face of the demon, towering over him, and then down at his stomach, and he knew fear was pointless and running, impossible. Death was inevitable. Even if he could fight the pain and get to his feet, he would die from his injuries.

"Is that what you want? To die?" he asked curiously, cocking his head to the side almost like a bird.

Eric thought about the question, as if there could be more than one possible answer to it, and then he shook his throbbing head from side to side and said, "No, sir." His voice was a gravelly whisper. "Are you going to kill me?"

The demon cocked his head to the side again, and looked at him with an intensity Eric had never seen before. It was a complicated look, filled with so many conflicting emotions that he couldn't pinpoint exactly what any of them meant. The demon sighed, a long and gusty sound. His eyes grew wide and clouded, and the pleasant cerulean fogged as a milky film swallowed them. He lifted his wrist to his mouth, biting down, and when he pulled it away, blood pooled on his skin. He slid closer, cradling his wrist as if he was trying not to let any of the blood to spill onto the snow, and before Eric could comprehend what was happening, the demon pressed his wound against Eric's lips and said, "Drink."

Eric squirmed and gasped. The movement sent shockwaves of pain coursing through his body. The demon cupped the back of his head, and held him firmly, with unyielding strength. Eric could feel the warm blood on his lips, seeping into his mouth, and his stomach rolled. But then he tasted it. Tangy and sweet and spicy. It was delicious and disgusting all at once, and Eric couldn't stop himself. He opened his mouth, latching onto the demon's wrist and drank, swallowing mouthfuls as quickly as he could.

The demon leaned in closer, but Eric didn't care. All he could think about was the mouthwatering blood that filled his mouth in a waterfall of goodness. Skin tingling warmth spread through his body.

The demon dropped his hand from the back of Eric's head, and then suddenly, his mouth was on Eric's neck. Eric felt the demon's teeth sink into his skin, but he didn't care. Nothing mattered except tasting the nectar of his blood.

It was when he pulled his arm away from Eric's mouth, that Eric noticed the demon's teeth were no longer in his neck. The disconnection felt cold, sending shivers along his skin. His eyes became heavy and drowsiness smothered him. He wanted to ask for more—demand more, anything to bring back the warmth and ease the pain of death, but his voice eluded him. He stared into the milky eyes, pleadingly, but the demon just smiled a little.

The shivers came quicker, and Eric's body convulsed from the cold. The pain in his stomach faded. It felt as if his mind couldn't take it anymore and had given up—shut down. Darkness grew around him. Then, despite all efforts, he couldn't keep his eyes open any longer, and they drifted shut.

CHAPTER 2

"Are we going to keep him?" a musical voice questioned, stirring Eric from his sleep.

Eric groaned, rolling onto his side. His throat was burning, parched. He smacked his mouth, trying to get some saliva moving to ease the painful flames that licked up his esophagus. His mouth was throbbing as if it had its own pulse. Eric scrubbed at his face and blinked awake. The room was dark, with only a soft flickering glow from a candle which rested on a table beside the bed that he occupied. But even in the dark, he knew that the bed was not his own, and this room was not in his ranch house. His heart jumped into his throat and he sprung up, sitting in the bed.

His eyes swept the room quickly. There was a small window in front of the bed, with light curtains pushed to the side, revealing that night had fallen. The inky black sky was streaked with approaching clouds, and small flakes of snow had begun to drift down. The room was small and welcoming, with whitewashed walls, and even hardwood flooring. The furniture was sparse but in good repair; a dresser nestled under the window, the small bedside table, and the bed.

And then he saw her—the angel with the musical voice.

Stunning. Her auburn locks cascaded over her shoulders in a waterfall of silk. His eyes trailed over her, taking in her lean body, her ample chest, and the way her woolen slacks hugged her curvy hips and long legs. Her face looked as if it had been sculpted from delicate clay, with doll lips and high cheekbones, and her eyes, big and chocolaty, were smiling at him.

"Who are you?" he whispered, his heart skipping a beat. "Am I dead?" *I must be,* he thought, because angels like this do not exist in life.

"No silly, you're not dead," she said with a giggle. "My name is Angelle." She sat down, perching on the edge of the bed, and smiled. Then she glanced towards the door. Eric followed her gaze, and his jaw dropped when his eyes found what she was looking at—the demon. "He's very handsome, Mitchell," she said excitedly. "I've never seen eyes like his before. They are so green, almost like grass in the springtime. We must keep him."

He didn't kill me. Panic clenched Eric's stomach, and he felt hot and cold and sick. His mind spun with questions. *Why? Why was he here? And where was here?* A pinprick of red burned in Mitchell's eyes as he watched Eric, closely, and thoroughly. *What does the demon want?* Eric did not know, but he also did not want to find out. His imagination ran wild with possibilities, torture being the one thing that his mind reached at the end of each avenue. He wanted to run, and he thought about it, but his legs wouldn't listen. He scrambled back, pressing himself against the wall, and he gripped at the blankets.

"Angelle, he's not a pet," the demon—Mitchell—said with a chuckle. "He may stay if he wishes, but he's not yours to keep." The way he spoke to her, it was as if he was speaking to a child, teaching her and guiding her.

Stay? Why would I want to stay with a demon? A soft *thump, thump, thump,* filled Eric's ears as the demon chuckled again, and for a moment, Eric's eyes locked onto his neck, where a throbbing vein pulsed rhythmically. The memory of the demon's tangy, sweet blood hit him, and his mouth watered. He kept his eyes fixed on the pulsing vein, unable to look away, and a thought dawned on him; Eric could see the demon's heartbeat in his throat, and he yearned for the blood that flowed through that vein. The hair on the back of his neck rose, and a rolling shiver prickled over Eric's shoulders. His eyes darted back and forth between the two strangers, and that's when he realized something else. There was no pain. His stomach felt … fine. Better than fine, actually. He dropped the blankets, pulled up his thin cotton shirt, and gasped. Not even a bruise.

"What have you done to me?" Eric breathed with a mix of wonder and fear in his voice.

Mitchell did not answer. He shifted uneasily, and for a split second, Eric thought the demon looked nervous. It seemed … odd, unreal, and it passed quickly, so quickly that Eric wasn't even sure that he had seen it.

A soft intake of breath that sounded like a sob brought Eric's attention back to Angelle. Her bottom lip jutted out, and her big brown eyes widened and drooped. It was so heartbreaking to see, that Eric couldn't stop himself. It was as if in that moment, all reason flew away, and as he looked at her, he forgot his fear, and he forgot that he should be dead. "Don't cry," he whispered. "Please don't."

"Promise you'll stay," she murmured, gazing at him through hooded eyes. "No matter what?"

Eric chuckled, mesmerized by the creature, and the burning in his throat grew. He knew he should be terrified, but oddly, he wasn't. He felt strong, stronger than he had ever felt before; his muscles vibrated with energy. The words slipped out without thought. "I promise," he said in a raspy voice. He brought a hand to his neck, rubbing down the center, trying to ease the blistering heat.

She tilted her head from side to side, searching his face for what, he did not know, but then, after a moment, her eyes lit up and she said, "Oh, you're hungry."

"Angelle," Mitchell snapped. He cut her a look of warning, and she shuddered slightly under his stare.

"I'm sorry," she whispered shyly, and in an incredibly quick motion, she was off the bed and standing before him. She kept her eyes cast down, as if she couldn't bear to look at the demon, and the way she trembled, Eric was certain she was frightened.

But the demon ... he smiled. It was a kind of adorning smile, one that a parent would give a child, and after a long minute, he said, "Go." Just that, one simple word. And in a blink, she was gone, and Eric was suddenly alone with the monster.

Mitchell closed the door with a soft click and leaned against it. His smile was gone; his lips drawn thin, in a straight white line, and he crossed his arms over his chest. Eric tried to keep calm, but in that moment, his heart was pounding into his throat. Eric did not consider himself a small man by any means, but near Mitchell, he felt it. There was something about Mitchell that commanded fear and intimidation. His presence filled the room like a thick fog, sucking out all rational sense.

"How are you feeling?" Mitchell asked, after staring at him for an excruciating and nerve racking long minute.

His deep, soothing voice calmed Eric's thumping heart. "What are you going to do with me?" he countered, unnerved by the bitterness that coated his tone, but he couldn't hold it back. This was cruel. All of it. Why hadn't the monster just killed him already? Or left him to die in the field? And more importantly, why didn't the idea of his impending death bother him?

Mitchell rolled his eyes. "Just answer the question, Son," he said with exasperation.

"Does the answer matter?" The question just flew out as if he had no filter. There was something about the way he had said *son*, almost gentle—tender—that made Eric furious. Rage grew inside him, simmering in his belly, and all he could see was red—literally. It was as if there was a film over his eyes tinting the world in scarlet. Fire licked up his throat, and his gums began to throb, pulsing in time with his racing heartbeat.

"There's no need to be frightened," Mitchell said softly. He pushed off of the door and closed the distance between them in a few long strides, taking a seat at the end of the bed.

"I'm not scared of you," Eric spat. Each word he spoke irritated his throat more, and again, he rubbed it, trying to calm the burn.

"Oh, no?" Mitchell chuckled and shook his head. His eyes fluttered shut, and his nostrils flared. When he turned back to Eric, two sharp fangs poked out from his lips. "I can smell it," he said, and he ran his tongue along the tips of his pointed teeth.

Eric stared at the teeth, sharp as knives, and he found them strangely intriguing. So many questions ran through his mind. Why fangs? Are they as sharp as they look? Did they hurt? But the question he asked was, "What are you?"

The question earned Eric a toothy smile, and the frown lines on Mitchell's forehead smoothed. "I'm the same as you." He paused, collecting his thoughts, and his smile vanished, although Eric didn't really consider that a bad thing. The fangs were fascinating, but they were also giving him the creeps, just a little. Mitchell sighed; then, and when, he looked at Eric, his eyes were pleading with him to understand. "Look, I didn't mean for this to happen. You weren't supposed to die. You weren't even supposed to know I was there."

"Clearly, I did not die," Eric said, and he was certain he was looking at the demon as if he was mad.

"Well…" Mitchell started, and then he dropped his eyes to the wooden floor. He ran his hands through his thick hair, and sighed. "In a way, you did die, Son. Please understand I had no choice. Even if I had managed to get you to a doctor before you passed, you would never have lived through your injuries."

Suddenly, things started to click together. His injuries were gone, and he was alive. Anger quickly bubbled up inside him, and Eric demanded, "What have you done to me?"

Mitchell looked up then, and his eyes washed red. "You are a vampire."

CHAPTER 3

Vampire. That one word awoke something in Eric, and a skin tingling chill rolled over his shoulders. *Vampire.* The word sounded strange—fake. Eric laughed. He couldn't stop it. It bubbled up and burst out of his mouth. But then something shifted in him, something dark, cold, and oddly exhilarating, and his laughter clogged in his throat. He jumped from the bed, landing nimbly on the balls of his feet, and ripped off his shirt, running his fingers over his hard abdomen, searching for any trace of damage.

Nothing. Absolutely nothing.

Impossible, a scared, little voice in his head whispered. All of this was impossible. He should be dead; Eric was certain of it. But as he examined his body, there wasn't even a scratch from where Sterling had landed, and his muscles were firmer, and more defined. "I'm not a vampire," Eric gaffed, still staring at his unmarked stomach. "They do not exist."

"They do and you are." There was amusement in Mitchell's deep voice as he spoke, but there was also an air of confidence. Eric couldn't just hear it; he could smell it, thick in the air. It was cool and assured, and it made Eric feel like a mad man. He listened to the demon's heartbeat,

13

drumming in regular thumps; it did not quicken, and he was certain it would if Mitchell was lying.

"Is this some kind of joke?" Eric questioned. His voice quivered slightly, and he wasn't sure if it was from fear or blinding anger. Both emotions were swirling together, binding as one. He narrowed his eyes, his jaw twitched, and heat rushed up his neck and settled in his cheeks.

"No," Mitchell replied, simply, as if that was enough of an answer. He sat on the edge of the bed motionless, staring at him intently, with his hands folded in his lap.

"The girl, Angelle, is she ...?" Eric couldn't finish the question, but the demon understood and nodded in confirmation. "Are there more?" he demanded, and Mitchell nodded again. The nods were maddening. Eric clenched his fists and began pacing the floor. The muscles along his neck and back went into a fit of spasms, rolling under his skin, and tensing as his anger rose to white-hot rage. "How long have I been sleeping?" Eric growled.

"An hour," he answered.

Eric stopped pacing and spun towards Mitchell. "Why did you do this to me?" he shouted. He had never felt anger like this before. It raged through him, like an angry bull. It was terrifying and invigorating, and it consumed him.

"I am not a monster, Mr. Carter," Mitchell said tightly. His lips were thin and his eyes, hard. He sat up straighter, and he rolled his shoulders back, making them look even larger. "You were dying, and I did what I could to make sure that did not happen. And if you recall, you did tell me that you did not want to die." He enunciated every syllable, with clipped precision, and the way he was looking at Eric was anything but amused.

"But you ... the myths ... you drink ..." his head felt as if it would explode. All the legends, all the tales, it was like waking from a dream only to find himself in a nightmare. And the persistent burning in his throat was driving him over the edge.

"Blood," Mitchell said with a nod, confirming the

14

statement, and his features softened a little.

Blood. The word made Eric's heart skip a beat, and his throat constricted. His gums began to pulsate, and he felt a pinch, a small tearing sensation, at the top of his mouth. He felt something slide down and then poke at his bottom lip, and he raised his hand to his mouth. He gasped when his fingers found two sharp fangs protruding from his gums. They were smooth, pointed, and Eric was certain they looked exactly like Mitchell's—deadly and intriguing.

Eric shuddered, and dropped down on the bed in shock. "What were you doing in my field?" he whispered, even though he was sure he already knew the answer.

Mitchell sighed, a gusty sound, and for a moment, Eric thought he wasn't going to answer, but then Mitchell said softly, "Hunting."

"Me?" Eric asked.

"Yes," Mitchell replied directly and plainly.

Eric looked at him then, searching his bright blue eyes for any hint of humanity. Mitchell's one word answer sounded cold, and callous, as if it were fact, or common even, to hunt humans, and Eric couldn't believe that anyone, demon or not, could be that cruel. But all he found in Mitchell's expression was confirmation, and his blood boiled. "So you did plan on killing me," Eric snarled savagely.

"No, I would only have taken what I needed to survive," Mitchell said. He reached over and patted Eric's knee. "You were not meant to die."

Eric batted the hand away, cringing at Mitchell's touch. *Not meant to die!* a voice in his head growled. Clearly, that was a lie. The demon had just openly admitted to hunting him. And hunting resulted in death. His skin buzzed, and his muscles coiled tightly. A growl, something savage and purely animalistic, rumbled in his throat, and his jaw ached from clenching it. Red flared all around him, fogging his vision, and washing everything his eyes touched in scarlet. "Christ, what's wrong with my eyes!" Eric shouted. It wasn't a question, but Mitchell answered it anyway.

Mitchell smiled a little. "Nothing is wrong with them, Son. It's normal for them to change when you are angry." His calm demeanor was infuriating, and Eric struggled to breathe through the constricting wrath building within his chest. "In time you will learn to control it."

"I'm not angry!" he shouted. He didn't know why he said it. Rage was coursing through him, smothering his senses, and coating his brain in a red-hot fog.

"I'm not sure I believe that this is your happy face," Mitchell said with a chuckle, and his eyes danced with humor.

The laughter was maddening, mocking, and it unlocked something in Eric. Heat rushed to his face, and he snarled. He launched at Mitchell, with a power and speed that he had not known was possible, and tackled him to the floor. Mitchell laughed again. It was a burst of velvety sound that died as quickly as it came out when Eric landed a punch squarely on his jaw. He felt the bone snap under his fist.

Mitchell's laughing eyes hardened, and suddenly they were cold and dangerous. With what seemed like nothing more than a flick of the wrist, he flung Eric off of him, and before Eric could really process what was happening, Mitchell's big hand was wrapped around his throat, pinning him against the wall. "Lesson number one, the older you are, the stronger you get," Mitchell said with barely contained fury. "Never pick a fight with an older vampire, because you will not win."

CHAPTER 4

There were four of them—vampires—including Mitchell. Or five, Eric figured, now that he was one of them, too. Lola was definitely his favorite, not that he was about to admit that to anyone, but he loved her spunk. She looked so sweet and quiet, but her looks were deceiving. She was outspoken, abrupt; she never sugar coated anything, and Eric found it refreshing. Especially since, for the last two weeks, Mitchell had been trying to hide all the downsides of being an immortal.

And there were downsides.

The first, and probably the hardest thing to swallow, was leaving his ranch and his family. The five of them had packed up and left the night Eric had become a vampire. Mitchell said it was better to just disappear. There was no point in drawing out the inevitable. It would only make it harder to let go in the end—and it would have to end. Sooner or later, his loved ones would notice that he did not age, and that would draw suspicion, and that suspicion would turn into fear. Eric wasn't sure if he agreed, but the truth was, he was also glad he hadn't had to try to explain where he was going and why he was leaving. His mother would never accept it.

But Willowberg wasn't so bad. It was bigger than he was used to, but not overwhelming, and the cool thing about Willowberg was that Mitchell had decided not to hide their true nature here. Turns out after seven hundred and something years, Mitchell was sick of moving around. He had purchased all of the establishments and the land that Willowberg rested on, offering the residents prices that they could not turn down. It was really a no brainer for the townspeople, because Mitchell didn't want any of them to move. They would all still live in their houses, and continue on with their work as they had before he had purchased everything. And he wasn't expecting anything from them, well, at least nothing that they knew about yet.

As Eric strolled down the main street, people stopped in their tracks to stare at him. Not that that was really a new thing; people, more precisely women, always stared at him. After all, he had been attractive before the change (not that he let that go to his head or anything) but now, everything about him was more defined. His muscles, his jaw, his eyes, his height. Except, Eric knew that wasn't the only reason they were staring. They were curious about the family that had just bought their town.

Eric was pretty sure that in a few hours, their curiosity would change to fear, and most likely, hatred. Even if he relished the idea of not hiding, he knew it probably wasn't going to turn out the way they hoped. People feared what they didn't understand. It was a fact of life. And Eric, for one, thought Mitchell's idea of living in peace with humans was more of a dream than anything. Eric was certain that as soon as the townspeople found out that his new family survived on drinking human blood, the town, and Mitchell's dream, would go up in flames.

They were set to expose themselves in just less than two hours. Angelle had been busy all morning setting up for the town meeting. It was to be held in their new home, and the chaotic preparations, well, more like the chaotic Angelle, had been so wired that Eric had needed to get out. She had more energy than any one person, vampire or not, should ever have. And she was driving him batty. She had this overly positive outlook on life, and most of the time, it was great, but right now … well, she was also a bundle of nerves about the meeting, and that made her chipper attitude even harder to handle.

Not ready to jump back into the pandemonium at home, and getting sick of all the stares, Eric veered off the main street, and took a small gravel path leading into the dense woodland surrounding Willowberg. He wasn't sure how long he walked, enjoying the chirping of the birds and the rustling of branches in the crisp breeze, when he stumbled upon a small snow covered clearing. Sunlight broke through the canopy of trees in stripes of gold.

It was just a small grove, nestled in the midst of a bunch of weeping willows, but to Eric, it felt like an oasis. A haven just for him. And for a minute, he longed for the peaceful wilderness that surrounded his ranch.

He ventured in, brushing aside the long, flowing branches, and leaned against one of the willow tree trunks. He closed his eyes, taking in deep, fresh breaths of the winter air, clearing his mind, and enjoyed the silence.

Fear. Its tantalizing aroma teased his nose and made his mouth water. It was sweet and sour and salty. His nostrils flared, and he breathed it in with long deep breaths. He opened his eyes lazily, scanning the area for the source of the mouthwatering scent.

Eric was starving. He was always starving. But with that scent wafting around him, he was extra-starving now.

"Who are you?" a girl's voice demanded from behind him, and the delicious scent increased. "What do you want from me?"

The sound of her voice was just as alluring as the scent of her fear. It was like an exquisite melody, filled with an intricate mix of chords, blending together perfectly. It was soft, sweet, and enchanting. Eric's heart raced, thumping loudly in his ears. He spun around, following the sound.

The girl stepped out from behind a tree, wisps of golden light radiated from her skin; her fear pulsed into the air as if it had its own heartbeat. She looked up at him, her cheeks wet with tears, and his breath caught in his throat.

She was beautiful.

Silky blood red ringlets cascaded over her shoulders and her eyes ... they were mesmerizing. The exact emerald green pigment of his own. Her slight frame had subtle curves, and the freckles that dotted the bridge of her nose were the cutest thing he had ever laid eyes on.

She made a sound. It was soft and sounded as if she gasped and moaned at the same time. He watched as her eyes raked over him, taking him in. She tugged her bottom lip between her teeth, nibbling on it lightly, and Eric heard her heartbeat pick up, drumming in time with his own.

And then the oddest thing happened—he moved. But it wasn't just that he moved, it was that he had absolutely no control over the movement. It was as if a rope was tied around him and he was being dragged, and suddenly, he was standing in front of her.

"Where am I?" she asked meekly, casting her eyes to the snow covered ground, and she took a small step back from him.

Eric ignored her question. "What's your name?" he breathed, completely and utterly in awe.

She blushed, her cheeks turning an adorable pink. "Megan Caldwell, sir."

He chuckled. "Please, do not call me sir." He wrinkled his nose, and she smiled a smile that lit up like sunshine. "It sounds so old." He extended his hand to her, and she laid her porcelain one in his palm. "I'm Eric. Eric Carter."

Suddenly there was a loud snap, and Eric sprang forwards. His head spun, and he felt slightly woozy. He leaned back against the willow, attempting to steady himself. He blinked a few times, focusing his double vision, and took in a deep, gusty breath. That's when he realized that Megan's soft hand was no longer clasped in his own. He scanned the clearing and took in deep breaths as he searched for her. Nothing.

Megan was gone.

Eric scrubbed at his face, trying to clear his head. There was no way she could just vanish. Not that quickly. She was just a human. He had smelled her blood, sweet and fresh, and he had heard it pumping through her veins. As he raked his hands over his face, he felt a dribble of wetness at the side of his mouth. Drool. *I dozed off,* he realized. *It was only a dream.* And in that moment, his heart burst into millions of sharp-edged pieces.

Eric stared blankly at the ground for some time before he pulled himself up, and started aimlessly down the path towards home. The whole thing had seemed so real. He could still smell Megan's sweet scent; still feel her fear clawing at his heart. All of it was so real. He had never had a dream like this before, and when he did dream, he rarely remembered a single detail once he woke up, but this was different. He could still feel her and see her, as if he was in two places at once. In the back of his mind, he could see her smile, hear her heartbeat …

"You're late," Lola said, as he walked through the door, and honestly, Eric didn't remember how he even got home. Lola stood in the kitchen, leaning against the icebox, with her arms crossed over her chest. She wore a soft pink cotton dress, and her thick blond hair flowed over her shoulders. She would have been gorgeous if it wasn't for the dirty look she was giving him right at that moment. Okay, Eric had to admit, she was still gorgeous with it, but it was really contradicting the sweet and innocent look she was trying to portray.

He cracked a half grin, trying to shake the bottomless feeling that had grown inside him. "Don't complain. My being late today will only make the times when I am early so much more special."

She choked on a laugh. "Oh, look at you. You think you are just so charming, don't you?"

Eric winked. "I don't think, I know." Lola laughed, grabbed a dishtowel from the counter, and threw it at him as he strolled into the kitchen. He caught it easily, dropping it on the table, before plopping down in a chair.

He saw Lola watching him from the corner of his eye, and after a moment, she blurted, "Are you okay? You look a bit ..." She paused, and wrinkled her nose, before continuing, "Lost."

Eric ran a hand through his hair, and then, with a sigh, he glanced at her. "I..." he started, but his voice sounded wrong. Empty and hoarse and rough. He cleared his throat, ran his fingers through his hair again, and plastered on a goofy smile that he hoped didn't look as fake as it felt. "I'm good."

Her blue eyes sparkled, and she arched a challenging brow. "You can talk to me, you know, ummm, if you want." It came out awkwardly, and by the way she was shifting back and forth, from one foot to the other, he was sure that she was probably regretting asking. Lola wasn't the *share your feelings* type.

Eric grinned. He couldn't stop it. He felt his lips curve, and his heartbeat picked up, thrumming against his ribcage. Lola sat down beside him, waiting for him to start talking. *Should I tell her?* he wondered. He wanted to. Really wanted to. Maybe if he talked about it, it would help.

He met her eyes, and her awkward smile widened to what he thought was supposed to be encouraging. He opened his mouth, the words on the tip of his tongue, but then panic gripped his chest, and his throat closed up. *What will she think of you?* a voice in the back of his mind questioned. He couldn't let her know that he had found the girl of his dreams—literally—in a dream. Lola would think he had lost his mind. He was supposed to be a vampire, a demon, not a lovesick fool pinning over an illusion.

So instead of letting the words he wanted to say come out, he shrugged and said, "Really, I'm fine."

It was clear as crystal that Lola didn't believe him, not for a second, but she didn't push the subject, and in Eric's opinion, she looked relieved to get out of the conversation. "Fine, then get your butt upstairs and get ready. The townspeople will be arriving any minute now."

CHAPTER 5

Angelle had outdone herself. As Eric walked through their colonial home, he hardly recognized it. The wooden floors gleamed with polish, and the Palladian windows were spotless. Not that the house had been dirty before, but it was extra-clean now. She had scrubbed down the wainscoting, the white looking brighter than before, and as he walked through the great room, he saw that she had constructed a makeshift platform with a podium, and before it were fifty or so chairs. Where she had found so many chairs so quickly, he couldn't even begin to imagine.

Eric took his time washing up and dressing for the meeting. Someone, Angelle, he assumed, had lain out a pair of black slacks and a white shirt for him on his bed. He could hear people arriving, chattering downstairs about the house, and curious murmurs about the sudden town meeting, and he knew he should hurry, but he just wasn't ready to face anyone yet. Although he was certain that Megan was just a figment of his imagination, his imagination seemed so much better than his life at the moment.

When he finally emerged from his room, he felt as if he had been beaten and drained, and for a split-second, he thought about just turning around and staying in bed for the rest of the day. The image of Megan was fading more and more every second, now, just a foggy outline in his memory, and all he wanted to do was to grip onto it—onto to her—and never let it go.

As soon as he stepped into the hallway, a caracole of scents bombarded him. Blood. So many different kinds of blood. Sweet, sour, tangy, spicy. He had never been in such close quarters with so many beating hearts before, and it made his throat burn. A crimson haze spread over his eyes, and the now familiar throb in his gums pulsated as his fangs begged to be released.

Eric shut his eyes and held his breath. He was already certain that this little meeting was going to be a disaster and showing up with blazing eyes and sharpened teeth would not help matters. He stood in the hallway, stiff as marble, as he attempted to get himself together. It was a task that was easier said than done. He pushed Megan out of his mind completely, focusing solely on not bursting downstairs and feasting on the closest neck he could find. After a long moment, the throbbing in his gums dissipated to a soft ache, and when he opened his eyes, the red fog was gone.

Eric sucked in a few breaths, testing his control. The delicious scents hit him again, and his heartbeat picked up, but his eyesight stayed normal. When he was certain that he could handle walking into a room filled with mouthwatering, fresh blood, he started down the hallway, with slow, small steps. This time, it was Angelle's voice that stopped him, holding him in place only a few paces from his room.

"You need to tell him, Mitch," Angelle's whispered voice floated around the corner of the hallway. "He needs to know what's happening."

"It may be just a dream, Angelle," Mitchell said, trying to sound casual, but Eric heard the strain in his voice. His curiosity peaked. Most of the time, Mitchell seemed emotionless, always wearing a mask, but with his tight voice … Eric couldn't help it. He stretched his hearing, needing to know what could possibly ruffle Mitchell's cool and calm persona.

"It's not," Lola hissed. "I'm sure of it. You didn't see Eric. You didn't hear his heart or smell his desire. He's found her." Her hasty tone was almost vicious.

Found who? Eric's heart stopped beating, and he strained his senses, anxious not to miss a beat of their conversation.

"I doubt that," Mitchell said. "He's only two weeks old."

"It could happen, and if he's not ready …" Angelle paused, and Eric could imagine the frown that marred her pretty little face. "He could make a mistake. She must be close, Mitch. If she wasn't, the dreams wouldn't have started yet."

There was a pause, and then Mitchell let out a deep sigh. "He knows the story. If it was her, I'm sure he would have put the pieces together."

Eric crept closer, desperately trying to keep quiet. What mistake? What do they know about the dream? What story? Could Megan be more than a dream? The questions burned through his mind, each one fighting over the other to be answered. And each one seemed ludicrous.

"Look, we don't have time for this right now," Mitchell said. "Everyone is waiting."

Eric took another small step, hoping they would keep talking. A floorboard creaked under his foot. He sucked in a breath, holding it, and trying not to make a sound.

"Hello, Eric," Mitchell called, his voice booming and tinted with annoyance.

The air rushed from Eric's lungs in a noisy burst. Why did he have to try and get closer? He glanced over his shoulder at his bedroom door hanging wide open, debated for a second about locking himself in there, but then knowing that was pointless and wouldn't hold against their strength, he let out a longing sigh, and ventured down the hallway.

"Sir," Eric said tightly and gave a small, stiff nod as Mitchell came into view. He was just around the corner, leaning against the banister at the top of the staircase.

Angelle and Lola were in front of him looking blameworthy, in Eric's opinion.

Mitchell arched a brow, but he didn't comment on Eric's formal greeting. His eyes scanned over Eric intently. "Are you ready?" he asked.

"Sure, where's Luke?" Eric asked. Angelle looked a bit jittery and nervous, and Eric shot her a questioning look, but she dropped her eyes and knotted her hands behind her back.

"He's mingling downstairs," Lola snapped, eyeing Mitchell with barely controlled rage.

Mitchell ignored her, giving Eric another hard look, and Eric was certain that Mitchell was assessing how much he had heard of the conversation. A pinprick of crimson began to spread over Mitchell's eyes, and his nostrils flared as he, Eric assumed, tried to get a fix on his emotions.

Eric steeled himself, tamping down all the questions and accusations that he wanted to let pour out of him. There was something about the way Mitchell was looking at him that made him sure that overhearing probably wasn't something he should admit to, at least not right now.

Mitchell must have bought his clueless act, because right then, his eyes faded back to blue, and he cracked a smile. "Let's get this over with."

CHAPTER 6

Luke wasn't mingling. Well, he was—kind of. He was milling about, talking to people, but when Eric saw his eyes, he knew Luke was doing more than engaging in small talk with the locals. His eyes were milky and cloudy, and he was walking from person to person, reciting the same speech over and over. "You will not be frightened, and you will welcome us." That's it. Just two simple commands, and then he would slip on to the next person.

Luke was a tall man, and bulky like Mitchell and himself. But he was the least intimidating of the three of them. He had this fatherly look to him, even if he had only been twenty-three when he had turned. There was something about him, the way he looked at people with his inquisitive hazel eyes that made people think he was wise beyond his years, and it also made people ... comfortable. Yes, Eric figured that was the best word to use. Comfortable. He had his shoulder length light brown hair tied at the nape of his neck, and he was dressed like the rest of them in black slacks and a white cotton shirt. Eric bet that Angelle had handpicked each of their attire for the meeting.

"That's your plan?" Eric hissed, as Mitchell ushered him to the platform. "You're just going to manipulate everyone."

"If it means living without hiding, then yes," Mitchell replied, casting him a hard look.

Eric narrowed his eyes, but bit his tongue on a bunch of nasty things he wanted to say. Mitchell wasn't a bad guy, and he wasn't usually this testy. Not that Eric would admit it, but he actually kind of liked Mitchell. Aside from the know-it-all, always-right attitude, Mitchell was a little awe-inspiring, and this little plan was sort of awe-inspiring, too. And it all bothered Eric. It would have been a lot easier to hate the man that had ended his life if he wasn't so ... so ... perfect.

According to Mitchell, the awe-inspiring, perfect thoughts thing was normal. A part of the change. It was common for new vampires to become a bit obsessed with their makers. It had something to do with them being made from the same blood, or was it that Mitchell was now his vampire father and family was important? Eric couldn't remember, and as he thought about it, he was pretty sure that Angelle had walked in during that lesson, and he had spent most of it admiring her silky auburn hair. But, whatever it was that made him feel like Mitchell was the most perfect person ever, it was definitely annoying.

Angelle and Lola glided into the crowd, helping Luke with the last few stragglers who had yet to be persuaded. Eric watched, amazed, as the two gorgeous creatures made mind control look like a dance. They spun gracefully from person to person, batting their eyes, giving men delicate, flirty touches. It was mesmerizing to watch. Before long, the girls and Luke took their places beside Eric, standing just behind Mitchell at the podium.

The meeting went off without a hitch. Eric stood behind Mitchell with his mouth hanging open the entire time. Mitchell explained to the townspeople how the new "tax" system would work. Basically, the humans were to willingly give their blood, and in return, Mitchell would allow them to stay in their homes and protect them as if they were his family. And each one of them thanked him. Actually thanked him for the opportunity he was providing. To Eric, it didn't seem like much of an *opportunity*. They were being forced to become walking meals. Eric didn't know whether to be sick or amazed at the whole thing.

After Mitchell finished his speech, his family left the platform and joined the humans for a reception. But Eric wasn't in the mood to chat. All he could think about was his bed, sleep, and Megan. So when no one was looking, he slipped out of the great room and went straight for his bed.

Sleep eluded him that night. Eric lay in bed, his eyes tightly shut, but yet, his brain would not rest. Megan's green eyes danced through his head, smiling at him and calling to him, but no matter how hard he tried, her eyes were the only thing that his brain would conjure.

He sifted through his memories, trying to recall what story Mitchell could have been referring to earlier as he spoke to Lola and Angelle. In the last two weeks since Eric had become a vampire, he had heard countless "stories." Mitchell called them *lessons*, except to Eric, they were more like boring and pointless rules. And since Eric had never really been a rules kind of person, he had promptly ignored them.

Now though, he wished he had listened.

Eric couldn't say how long he had lain there, when he heard the knock at his door. "Eric?" Mitchell called from behind his bedroom door. Eric groaned, and the door slid open. "I heard that," his father said with a chuckle.

Eric sat up in bed and scrubbed at his face. "I was sleeping," he said, trying to sound groggy and hoping Mitchell would just go away.

He didn't. Mitchell closed the door with a soft click and crossed the room, sitting down in the armchair beside the window. He leaned forwards, resting his elbows on his knees, and his chin in his hands. "Was it her?" he asked elusively, his voice a confusing mix of pain and happiness.

"What are you talking about?" Eric was sure he was

looking at Mitchell as if he was a mad man. He was really starting to think that he would never get used to Mitchell's direct and slightly elusive attitude. The way he spoke, even when asking a question, was as if everything was a secret. Except this time, Eric knew exactly what Mitchell was asking, but his gut was telling him to keep his mouth shut and play dumb.

"Did she have the mark?" Mitchell asked, his eyes boring into Eric so intently that he felt as if Mitchell was actually seeing into his brain.

"You know I was just sleeping, right?" Eric asked. He didn't understand why, but he didn't want to share Megan. He just didn't. Not with anyone. At this point, he was certain that they were all just speculating, at what, he really wasn't sure, but they didn't really know anything—yet.

"Oh, give it up, Eric," Mitchell said. "You weren't sleeping. Did she have the mark on her neck?"

Eric threw up his hands, exasperated, this time really having no idea what Mitchell was asking. "What mark?"

Mitchell eyed him again, and Eric figured that Mitchell had finally realized that Eric had no idea what he was talking about, because he let out a deep sigh and leaned back in the chair, letting his arms dangle over the armrests. "Eric, I'm asking if she had the soul's mark." His tone was crisp and clipped. "But clearly, you must not have been listening when I told you about it."

A frustrated growl rumbled through Eric. "Well, tell me now," he said through clenched teeth. "What is the soul's mark and what does it have to do with Megan?" *Darn it! Why did I say her name!*

Mitchell arched an eyebrow and smirked. "Megan?" he questioned.

Eric growled in frustration, and all he could see was red. "Just get on with it," he spat venomously. Mitchell's smirk was irksome. Maddening.

Mitchell sighed, and shook his head in disappointment at Eric's lack of control, Eric assumed, because the look he was getting was definitely the one Mitchell gave when he lost control over his emotions.

After what felt like ages, Mitchell cleared his throat and said, "It's a witch's curse. As I told you before, about fourteen-hundred years ago, a vampire killed a witch's lover. Out of revenge, she stripped all vampires of their souls, leaving them as soulless monsters with no humanity. Mother Nature corrected it. She linked our missing souls to our soulmates through the soul's mark, the alchemy symbol for soul, which would have appeared on our soulmates necks when we became vampires. The mark gives us a connection to our humanity and ultimately to them." He said the whole thing in one breath with a methodical air, as if he was reading a well-rehearsed speech.

Eric's throat was tight and his mouth, dry. There was something in Mitchell's little speech that sounded vaguely familiar, and Eric was pretty sure he should be drawing some kind of connection, but he wasn't. His mind was a blank slate. "What does this have to do with my dream?" he asked.

Mitchell smiled—a little. "Everything … and possibly nothing at all."

CHAPTER 7

Eric jumped up from the bed and advanced on Mitchell, towering over him as he sat, relaxed, in the armchair. "Do you realize how infuriating you are?" he yelled down at Mitchell. "Can't you just give me a straight answer? Why does everything have to be a bloody secret with you?"

"Calm down, Son," Mitchell said, and rolled his eyes.

But Eric couldn't. Suddenly, terror spiked through him, rushing through his veins in a burst of heat. Lightheadedness overtook him, and he stumbled. Eric reached out, gripping onto the window ledge as he fought against the dizzying blast. His head spun, his heart raced, and darkness began seeping in around the edge of his vision. He blinked furiously, fighting against the gray fog that was settling over his eyes.

Someone screamed. It was loud and quiet all at once. An echo vibrating through his brain. And it was familiar. The voice, even with the panicked screams, sent shivers and sparks through his body. *Megan.*

"Eric," Mitchell said, his voice filled with concern. He shot out of his chair and began inching towards Eric slowly, cautiously, as if he was scared to move too fast.

Eric opened his mouth to say something, but his voice

lodged in his throat. Megan screamed again and again and again, and in the back of his mind, Eric swore he could see her running. Her face was tear stained, and her hair was flying wildly around her shoulders. Her eyes were wide and terrified, and she kept glancing over her shoulder as if someone was chasing her.

She stumbled, falling to her knees, and then clenched her hands to her chest. Looming shadows were closing in on her. Big, dark figures, wearing cloaks. "They're going to hurt her," Eric blurted. What was happening to him? How could he be seeing her as if he was standing right in front of her? The image in his mind was so crisp that it was as if he could reach out and touch her.

"Who?" Mitchell demanded, and for half a second, Eric looked at him, and when he did, he was sure he saw trepidation in Mitchell's eyes.

"The ... the ... I don't know," Eric wailed in frustration. "She fell, and there are shadows ..." Eric caught a glimpse of a hand, and he growled. "They have bows and arrows."

Mitchell grabbed his shoulders, and shook him roughly. "Eric, you have to stop thinking about her. You're going to pull her to you."

"I have to help her!" Eric shouted, thrashing about as he tried, unsuccessfully, to get Mitchell's hands off of him. All at once, he drew the lines that he hadn't been able to connect before. She was real. She was his. And someone was trying to hurt her. He didn't know why or how he knew this, but he did. He could feel it in his bones, in his heart, in his essence. She was his soulmate.

As if Megan knew he was watching, in that moment of realization, she shifted her head, giving him a clear view of her neck, and it was there—the mark—a black figure eight with a solid line passing behind the bottom loop. *His soul's mark.*

"Then you have to let her go," Mitchell said sternly. "She needs to keep running. Trust me." There was desperation in his voice, as if he was begging Eric to listen.

"You need to stop watching and let her run." He paused for a second, and his eyes misted. "Please stop," Mitchell pleaded.

But Eric couldn't. He had no control over whatever was happening. He didn't understand it. Why couldn't Mitchell see that? Eric watched helplessly as Megan's body began to separate, as if her spirit was leaving her, and suddenly a wavy image of her floated above as her body collapsed to the ground.

Eric cried out, terrified, and his body began to shake.

"Mr. Carter?" Megan screamed, panicked. Her voice filled the room, and her erratic heartbeat hit Eric's ears like a punch in the gut. He swiveled his head, following the sound, and he sucked in a startled breath. Her green eyes were piercing and full of alarm, and her blood red curls, untamed.

Mitchell cursed. And then, in a swift motion, he grabbed Eric's chin and twisted, and everything went black.

****

Eric woke up with a start. His neck snapped and popped, and he could feel his spine piecing together under his skin. His neck muscles tightened, and with another uncomfortable snap, they loosened again. He gasped, and the air burned through his lungs as if he had been holding his breath for hours. His eyes began to water, and he scrubbed at his face. *What the hell happened?*

"Eric, I want you to check on Megan," Mitchell said.

Eric dropped his hands from his face, and shifted his gaze to Mitchell. He was sitting at the edge of his bed, with a grim expression, and he wouldn't meet Eric's eyes.

In a split second, everything came racing back. The soul's mark. The curse. Megan. She had been scared. She had been here. His eyes blazed, and his fangs snapped down. "What did you do?" Eric demanded.

Mitchell cringed, and shuffled around on the bed

uncomfortably. After a moment, he took a deep breath and said in a rush, "You pulled her spirit here, so I broke your neck."

"You what!" Eric seethed.

"I needed to break the connection. If someone was chasing her, she had to keep running, and she couldn't do that if she wasn't in her body," Mitchell said, as if it was simple logic.

"Where is she?" The words came out in a growl, and Eric glared at Mitchell. *I can't believe he broke my neck!*

"I don't know," Mitchell said, his calm and controlled demeanor back in place. He tossed up his hands and waved them around. "Hence, why I want you to check on her."

"How in the hell am I supposed to do that if you don't even know where she is? She was just here!" Eric had seen her. She had been here which meant, obviously, that no one was chasing her.

Mitchell nodded. "In a way, yes. I'll explain it all, but first you need to see if she is okay. Take a deep breath, close your eyes, and look for her."

Eric did what he was told for two reasons. One: he really wanted to make sure Megan wasn't just an illusion. And two: Mitchell was getting annoyed, and that never ended well.

When Eric closed his eyes, Mitchell said, "Now, when you find her, try to pick out anything around her that will help you track her location. If she falls again, drop the thought. I don't want you bringing her back here in case she is still in trouble. She needs to stay with her body."

It made no sense to Eric, but he did as he was told. He couldn't say how long he sat there trying to visualize Megan. It felt like hours, but no matter how hard he thought about her, he saw nothing. Only blackness. He was just about to give up when he heard a soft whimper. There was some crunching, as if someone was walking on gravel, and then a thud. A gasp and skin slapping skin.

"Eric, stop!" Mitchell said. "Stop!"

CHAPTER 8

The sun rose and then it set, and still Eric didn't have any answers. Not that Mitchell hadn't tried to give them, he had. It was just that Eric couldn't concentrate. He couldn't seem to wrap his head around the idea that the girl of his dreams was actually real, alive, and out there somewhere. And it really didn't help that every five minutes Megan was screaming, and each time she did, it wrecked havoc on his heart. Mitchell said it was a good thing that she was screaming. It meant that she was still alive, but Eric couldn't stand her feeling so scared.

"So you don't have any idea where she is?" Lola asked for at least the hundredth time.

"No," Eric said, and he ran his hands through his hair. Luke, Lola, Angelle, and Mitchell sat around the round oak kitchen table staring at him. They were all giving him a look that said they didn't believe him. Did they really think he would be sitting here with them if he knew where she was?

"Well, you need to find her," Angelle chirped, as if it was the first time it had been said.

When Mitchell said that the soul's mark gave a vampire a connection to their soulmate, he hadn't been lying. From what Eric understood, his soul was in Megan, and the mark allowed him to use his soul to, in a sense, push hers out of her body. When that happened, he could then call her to him. Mitchell explained that this usually only happened while the vampire and soulmate were asleep, like a vivid dream.

In the dream state, Eric could also use the mark to force his soul out of her body for a limited amount of time. And this was exactly what Mitchell wanted him to do. If Eric did, then he would appear where she was, and he might be able to narrow down her physical location.

"I can't try if we are both awake, now can I?" Eric snapped, frustrated and annoyed, and maybe a little hungry.

Since Eric seemed to have absolutely no self-control, Mitchell had insisted that he needed to learn some. He claimed that it would help find Megan, and self-control was allegedly the only way their race could survive, although Eric thought his father was just trying to punish him. For what, he didn't know, but there always seemed to be a reason. All he wanted to do was find Megan, but each time he did, Mitchell would force him to stop, and Eric was really getting tired of having a broken neck. Eric knew Mitchell was doing it to keep Megan safe. The only times he had been able to grip onto her spirit was when she was running for her life, but still, it was infuriating.

They had wandered around Willowberg for ten hours in the frigid snow while Mitchell introduced him to fear, love, and anger. Forcing the emotions on him and making him breathe in the scents that came from them. And then, when Eric thought he would surely die of starvation, Mitchell had forced him to walk away. Walk away from the pounding hearts, the sound of blood quickening in their veins, and not give in to the temptation.

It had been the worst lesson yet. There was something about the strong emotions that made the blood sweeter. Alluring. Magical. Just the thought of it made his teeth sharpen, ripping through his gums like thick needles through flesh. And with all the insane emotions he was feeling with

Megan's fear rupturing inside him, mixed with the lesson, he was famished.

But the lesson, not that Eric would ever tell Mitchell, had worked. When Megan screamed, it was easier to keep control and let her run instead of bringing her to him.

"You actually saw her?" Luke asked Mitchell, his hazel eyes questioning.

"No," Mitchell said, shaking his head. "I didn't have time to look. But she was here, and as soon as I heard her voice, I *stopped* him."

"How?" Luke asked simply, before Eric had a chance to spit out exactly what he thought of Mitchell *stopping* him.

"Before the fire ..." Mitchell started, and then stopped, swallowing hard. He glanced out the window, but by the look on his face, Eric was pretty sure Mitchell wasn't actually seeing anything. The silence grew thick in the air, and Eric noticed that the others were looking at Mitchell with deep sympathy.

"Mitch, you don't have to talk about her," Angelle said, breaking the awkward stretch of silence. She pulled her chair closer to him and wrapped an arm around his shoulder, giving him a squeeze.

Mitchell smiled, a sad kind of smile, and then he took a deep breath, releasing it slowly. "When Amelia was scared, when her emotions were running wild, I could latch onto her and pull her out while we were awake. When I did, well she appeared as herself, and anyone around could see her, touch her, as if she was really, fully there."

Eric blinked, and then blinked again. *What?* Who was Amelia? What fire? How many things did he not know? Or maybe the better question was how many of Mitchell's lessons had he ignored?

"She used your vampiric energy to gain substance," Lola said matter-of-factly. Everyone looked at her then, and she shrugged. "What? After she died, I did some research about the connection. It's more common than you think, especially when the connection is strong."

They were all still gaping at Lola as if they had never seen her before, when Eric blurted, "Who is Amelia?"

Mitchell opened his mouth to speak, but to Eric's amazement, he closed it just as quickly. For the first time since Eric met him, Mitchell looked ... broken. Utterly and completely broken. There was no mask. His emotions were thick in the air; cold, broken, and empty. It was as if a piece of him died at the mention of her name, but behind the brokenness, Eric also caught something else, self-loathing and a burning hatred. Even Eric knew that was a dangerous mixture.

"She's Mitchell's soulmate," Angelle said. She whispered a few soothing notes in Mitchell's ear and rubbed his shoulder, her arm still wrapped tightly around him, before she continued. "She was burned as a witch just over three-hundred years ago, and he hasn't been able to find her since."

"She died, and you're still looking?" Eric said it as a question, because well, it was. Mitchell smiled at him, or that's what Eric thought it was supposed it be. It looked more like a freaked-out sneer than a smile.

"Eric, no human really dies," Mitchell said, his voice thick with emotion. "Their body may, but the soul never does. Even if you don't find Megan in this lifetime, she'll come back to you in another." He offered another scary looking smile, and Eric cringed.

Not find Megan? That wasn't a scenario that Eric wanted to think about. It was right then that he decided what he would do. The others continued on, telling him about the mark and some kind of bond that happens after a human gets bitten by their vampire soulmate, but Eric wasn't listening. No, he was too busy forming a plan. A plan to find Megan before whatever, or whoever, was after her found her first.

CHAPTER 9

Eric was being held—restrained. He figured it was his own fault; he should never have attempted to come up with a plan while the others had been trying to explain what was happening to him. Mitchell had said it was evident, written clearly across Eric's face. So ... Mitchell had locked him away, supposedly to stop Eric from doing anything rash and impulsive. Mitchell claimed it was just until they all knew what they were dealing with, but Eric didn't care why.

The cellar was damp and dark, and the chains that kept Eric pinned to the wall were cold. But he hardly noticed any of it. All he had really noticed for the last three days was the relentless tug around his heart. Three excruciatingly long days. And each day, Megan's fear was stronger. And the stronger it got, the harder it was to stay civil. He wanted to go a rampage, killing anyone that stood in his way. He had never felt so useless before. But right now, that's exactly how he felt. Useless.

"Eric, this is for your own good," Mitchell said. He had been sitting in front of Eric, blabbing on and on about soulmates, and dreams, and God only knows what else for hours now. "You'll only put her in more danger by chasing her."

"You don't know anything!" Eric snarled, yanking against the chains. He wanted to kill Mitchell—literally. All

41

he could think about was ripping out his throat. And the more he thought about it, the more he wanted to break the chains, drive his hand through Mitchell's chest, and tear out his heart. He felt like a wild animal, savage and ruthless, and although he knew *this* was not him, he relished the thought of watching Mitchell's body fall in a lifeless heap at his feet.

Mitchell rose from his chair, and his eyes flashed red. "I've spent seven hundred years dealing with this bond, Eric. If you're not thinking clearly, you'll hurt her. You could even kill her."

"You're insane," Eric hissed. Kill her. He wouldn't hurt her. Never.

Mitchell tossed his hands up in exasperation, and started pacing the dirt cellar floor. "I'm trying to help you. You're too young for this."

"How can you tell me she's real, and then lock me up like a rabid dog?" Eric spat, barely hearing Mitchell's pleas. "I thought you cared about me. I thought I was your family."

"I do care, Eric," Mitchell said softly, and then he sighed, a sad kind of sound. "I know you don't understand, but it is because I care that I can't let you run after her until you know where she is, and what's chasing her. You'll only make things worse."

"I hate you!" Eric yelled. As soon as the words left his mouth, he regretted them. Mitchell looked ... well, he looked like Eric had physically punched him, and it was awful. Completely and utterly awful. He may want Mitchell dead, but he also loved him. It was the most confusing mix of emotions that Eric had ever felt.

Mitchell dropped down into a chair and scrubbed at his face as he whispered, "I know."

****

Lola brought Eric dinner that night. It was a blonde with bright blue eyes, and she was overly willing to donate her blood. She even urged him to take more than he needed, and Eric was pretty sure she would have let him drain every last drop of blood she held within her body if she had thought it would make him happy.

She was curled up on the dirt floor beside him, her head resting on his bare chest. "Will you please leave," Eric said through gritted teeth, again. He lifted his shoulder from the wall with a jerk, in an attempt to dislodge her head from his chest. It didn't work.

She shifted her cheek so she could glance up at him through sad, sleepy eyes. "Why don't you like me?" she asked, pouting. She ran a finger up and down his chest, playing with the top of his slacks before dragging her nail back up again.

Eric just shrugged. What was he supposed to say? *I don't like you because you are just a meal. You are food, that's it.* It sounded overly harsh, even if it was the truth. What did these humans expect? Did they really think they could be more than a handy meal? And really, did the girl miss the fact that he was chained to a wall? She had been delivered to a prisoner (well, not really a prisoner, but she didn't know that) and she was begging for more of him. Whatever manipulation Lola had used, she had definitely gone overboard.

"Am I not good enough for you?" she said, her voice whiney and overly grating.

"What?" he asked distractedly, and nudged her head again, but this time she wrapped an arm around him, holding him tightly to her. He wished that Lola would come back and take her away, because small talk with food was really, really not something he wanted to do.

"Is there someone else?" she whispered, nuzzling against him, her breath warm against his skin, and she lightly trailed her fingers down his chest again.

Eric groaned loudly. He was going to wring Lola's scrawny little neck the next time he saw her. If this was her idea of a joke, brainwashing some poor girl to offer herself to him in ways that she shouldn't even think of offering to anyone but her husband, he would throttle her.

"Mr. Carter?" Eric cringed at the sharp tone. *Megan*. He reluctantly followed the sound, glancing up, certain that he would see anger in those pretty green eyes.

He did.

Her eyes were bright and full of fury. He should have known she would pop up now. Since Mitchell had put him here, she seemed to only show up when he was doing something he did not want her to see, or when she was terrified and running for her life. She hadn't been sleeping much, too scared to close her eyes, but over the last few days ... well, she had found him in a few embarrassing situations.

And of course, like every other time she had appeared, Mitchell wasn't here to see her. Eric was certain that if Mitchell could just see Megan, he would let him go.

"Hello, Megan," Luke's voice boomed from the doorway, before Eric could even open his mouth.

Megan spun on her heels, her hands on her hips. "Who are you? Why are you in my dream?" she blurted in a frenzy. Then she turned back to Eric, and her eyes shimmered with angry tears. "Who is that girl all over you, Mr. Carter?" she demanded, with a little stomp of her foot.

"I should ask you that. This is your dream," Eric said, and chuckled. He couldn't help it. Megan was just so darn cute when she was angry. She pursed her lips and put her hands back on her hips, tapping her foot and waiting for more of an answer. *If she only knew that I was real,* Eric thought, *she would probably try to stake me.* Because with the look she was giving him, well, Eric wasn't sure if she was going to try to kill him or go after his meal.

Luke swept past Megan. "I'm a friend of Eric's, and she is no one." He bent down, scooping the girl up in his arms, and whispered so softly that only Eric could hear him, "Ask her where she is. I'll be back in a moment." Luke met his eyes, staring at him intently for a moment, and then he left, taking the girl with him.

Once Luke was gone, Eric was sure Megan was going to yell at him. She looked like she wanted to, but she didn't. She just stood there, with narrowed eyes, and her hands still on her hips, and that was even worse. He would have preferred to hear all the hateful things she was thinking. To know how badly he had messed up, even if he really hadn't done anything. Instead, she just glared, and the silence between them was so thick that Eric could scarcely breathe.

Finally, after an eternally long moment, she sighed and shook her head. "Mr. Carter, why in the world are you chained to that wall again?"

"Like I said before, it's your dream, you tell me," he said hastily, frustrated. Eric had decided not to tell her the truth yet, and holding it back was brutal. He wanted to wait and tell her everything in person. In person, she would believe it, he was certain, but in a dream ... he knew she wouldn't.

Megan rolled her eyes. "Well, I guess I must fix it then." She scanned the room, searching, and when she spotted the key ring hanging by the door, she walked over to it and lifted the keys off the hook. She turned back to him triumphantly, dangling the keys from a finger.

Megan took her time crossing the few steps to him, and her hand trembled slightly as she began unlocking the chains. Eric watched, mesmerized. He could hear her heartbeat and smell the sweetness of her skin. He knew she was an illusion, she wasn't really there, but she was so real. And with her so close, leaning over him as she unlocked the shackles, he could even feel the heat from her skin. It was magic, plain and simple, magic.

"I was hoping I would dream of you again," she murmured, as the last chain fell away.

Eric grinned, and he almost giggled—almost. "Really?" he asked, as a little voice in his head shouted, *she wanted to see me again!*

"Well, yes ..." she blushed, and dropped her eyes. But then she screamed. It rang, shrill and sharp. And just as

45

quickly as she had appeared, she was gone. Vanished without a trace, as if she had never been there to start with.

Megan screamed again, and a loud metallic clatter resonated around his brain. The sound was agony to his ears, and his heart skipped a beat. Eric gritted his teeth, fighting to block out Megan's screams. He could feel her awake and sensed that she was running, fearing her life, and he had to keep her that way.

Awake and running.

Eric bolted towards the door, and a wave of fear hit him, knocking him off balance. He gripped onto it, the wood snapping within his hands, as he forced himself to stay awake, and keep her spirit in her body.

CHAPTER 10

Luke wasn't happy. He stood in the doorway, blocking Eric's exit, with his arms crossed and his jaw flexed. "Where did she go?" he asked coarsely, as Eric tried to get a grip on himself, and push Megan from his mind.

"She woke up," Eric said through gasping breaths. "She's running." He leaned against the wall, slouched over with his hands on his bent knees, sucking in mouthfuls of air, as Megan's panic flood through him. At times like this, when she was this scared, it felt as if her emotions were actually his. It was as if her terror was coursing through his body, and the urge to run and hide was overwhelming.

If Luke noticed how much Eric was struggling to keep control over his own reality, he didn't let on. He walked into the room, slamming what was left of the splintered door shut, and grabbed Eric by the arm. He dragged Eric over to one of the chairs, and deposited him in it. "Did you ask her where she was this time?" he asked once he had taken a seat in a chair across from Eric. Luke hunched forwards, resting his elbows on his knees.

Eric shook his head from side to side. "No, there wasn't enough time." But then, there never was enough time. Since the so-called *dreams* started, Megan had never stayed with him long.

Luke nodded, just a slight dip of his head, and he waited,

staring at Eric with those inquisitive hazel eyes. Eric didn't know what Luke was waiting for, or what he was supposed to say. So instead of saying anything, he held Luke's stare, and to Eric's surprise, the staring contest helped. It gave him something to focus on, and made it easier to handle Megan's racing heart, which had now become a permanent fixture in the back of his mind.

Luke blinked first. "You need to stop fighting with Mitchell." There was a small curve to his lips, as if he knew how impossible that statement was.

"What do you care?" Eric challenged, confused by the look Luke was giving him. He leaned back in the uncomfortable wooden chair and crossed his arms over his chest. "He obviously doesn't."

Luke's expression changed in a beat. He eyed Eric sternly, furrowing his brow. "Eric, you're his first child. He's trying."

"He's a monster!" Eric yelled, jumping to his feet, and started pacing. He clenched his fists, and heat rushed up his neck, settling into his cheeks. "He doesn't give a crap about me, or anyone. He's going to let Megan die!" Eric knew it wasn't entirely true. He knew that Mitchell and Luke, and well, all of them, were just trying to help him. Racing out the door and searching for someone that could be anywhere wasn't the smartest thing to do, but it was the only thing he could think of. It was as if his soul was begging him to find her. A constant tug at his body, urging him to abandon everything, and do nothing but search. Every fiber, every cell, every single piece of his body and mind longed for her.

"You're wrong," Luke said, not unkindly. "He does care. Look ..." Luke ran his hand through his hair and scrubbed at his face. "You know that Lola is my soulmate, right?" he asked after a minute.

That threw Eric for a loop. "What?" he blurted, stopping his relentless pacing, and looked at Luke. He knew they were *together*. It wasn't as if they had hid it, but he had never really considered that any of the others had found their soulmates. If they had, they would have understood that he couldn't stay here. They would help him, not *restrain* him. They would let him search.

Luke's eyebrows rose. "Come on, you must have noticed her mark. She's my soulmate."

Eric tried to remember if he had ever noticed Lola's mark. She always had her hair down, covering her neck, and in all honesty, he couldn't say if he had ever seen it. If he had, he was sure he would have asked about it. *Wouldn't I?*

"Mitchell isn't really the best at explain things," Luke continued. "He's locked you up here because he doesn't know what to do. He doesn't know how to make you understand what finding her means or what can happen when you do. And with you refusing to talk to him …" Luke smirked, and right then, Eric was pretty sure Luke knew just how infuriating Mitchell could be, "… and showing him you have no control over your emotions … well, you'll be stuck here until you show him you're ready for this."

"Ready for what, exactly?" Eric asked. *Maybe Luke wasn't so bad.* Maybe he actually wanted to help. He looked like he did, and he also looked like he knew exactly how Eric felt.

Luke smiled approvingly, and Eric figured that he had asked the right question. "Ready for the bond. It can change you; make you do things that you never would have thought possible. I've seen vampires take their own lives because of it. And Eric, there's no coming back for a vampire." Eric shuddered inwardly as he listened. There was an ominous tone to Luke's timbre, as if he had harnessed a storm and channeled it into his voice, making his words sound harsh, and dangerously true. "You have, or could have, complete control over that girl. You could make her do things, control her every thought, every move. It can ruin you and ruin her."

Eric stifled a groan. "You make just about as much sense as Mitchell. I would never try to control someone."

"You say that now, but trust me, it will change."

"Is there a point here?" Eric asked, plopping back down in his chair. He scratched at his head, trying to make sense out of what Luke was saying.

"Now," Luke said, dropping his voice to a whisper so low, that Eric had to strain to hear. "If you are ready to pretend like you are not some psychopath on a mission, I believe I can convince Mitchell that you do not need to be kept down here."

Eric scrunched his brow, confused. "Pretend?"

Luke put a finger to his lips and *shushed* him. Actually *shushed* him, and Eric almost laughed—almost. "Yes," he whispered with a nod, and his eyes danced with amusement. When he continued, his voice was booming loud. "Didn't you just say that you thought Mitchell was right and you were willing to wait?"

"Err ... okay?" Eric said it as if it was a question, because, well, it kind of was. Talk about confusing. Eric wasn't sure what to think. Was Luke really trying to break him out so he could search for Megan?

Luke winked, and rose from his chair. "Alright then, but I don't want you sneaking out when we aren't looking. Stick to what you just told me. You don't want to put her in more danger by finding her." Luke was practically shouting their conversation for Mitchell's benefit, Eric figured, and it took everything Eric had in him not to burst out laughing.

To say Mitchell was relieved to see him was a definite understatement. As soon as Eric cleared the last step leading upstairs, he was wrapped in a bone-breaking bear hug.

Luke did most of the talking; reiterating the conversation, explaining how Eric finally understood, and he even apologized profusely on Eric's behalf for worrying everyone. Each time Eric tried to say something, anything, Luke would just talk over him. In no time, Luke was ushering Eric up another flight of stairs, and pushing him down the hallway into Eric's bedroom.

"Now, you remember what I said, no sneaking out,"

Luke said, and then he pulled the door shut, leaving Eric alone.

CHAPTER 11

Eric stared at the ground so far below him. His heart was racing, and his hands began to sweat. Theoretically, he knew that the jump could not hurt him, but his brain was still stuck on being human. And this three-story jump would hurt a human.

Just jump, his brain commanded, but his feet didn't listen, so he closed his eyes, figuring that if he couldn't see the ground so far below, it may make it easier. It didn't.

It wasn't until he heard the shuffling outside his bedroom door that Eric flung himself through the open window. He hit the ground with a quiet thud, landing on his feet, and he took off running as fast as he could.

The sun was just starting to rise, soaking the cloud covered horizon with pinks and oranges. It was a cool morning, and flakes of snow fell all around him as he ran. He knew he needed to get as much distance between him and his family as fast as possible. If he didn't, and they caught him, he was certain they would drag him back. Being the youngest had its downsides. They were all stronger than he was, and so much faster. His only hope was a head start.

Mitchell thought that Megan was close. He said that the dreams wouldn't be happening so soon if she wasn't. The problem was Mitchell thought it was better to wait, and try to get a lock on her location. But Eric just couldn't sit back and wait. Not now. Not when he knew she was more than just a dream. And definitely not with her so scared. He had no choice. He had to find her. Even now, he could feel her fear. It was a constant tug, a pull on his essence, and it was a struggle to stay lucid.

He launched himself into the forest, heading east at full speed. Eric knew that Mitchell meant well, but he couldn't stand by and wait. Mitchell was going on his own experience with Amelia. He had explained that she had been burned at the stake because of him, because of the dreams. That's why she had been accused of witchcraft in the first place, but this ... this was different. Eric was certain that Megan was being hunted. Why else would there be people chasing her with bows and arrows, if not to kill her?

Okay, so maybe it wasn't so different. Technically, people had been hunting Amelia as a witch, and now Megan was being hunted ...

Eric ran for two hours without even a glance over his shoulder before he allowed himself to stop. He scaled a tree, getting out of sight, and perched on the highest branch that would hold his weight. He scanned the forest below him for any sign of Mitchell. He scrutinized every whisper of wind that brushed through the dry, snowy branches, every crunch of snow, every squirrel and bird, until he was certain that none of the sounds came from his family and no one had followed him.

Exhaling a pent-up breath that he hadn't even known he was holding in, Eric leaned back against the tree, his legs dangling on either side of the branch, and closed his eyes for just a moment.

The air was frigid and crisp. Eric sucked in a few deep breaths, watching his breath puff out in smoky clouds. He had never been much of a planner and now was no different, he guessed, since he really hadn't thought of much more than getting out of the house undetected. He looked at the snow-covered ground shimmering below him under the brilliant sun, and raked his hands through his hair.

Plan ... Plan ... Plan ... I need a plan. He knew he couldn't just sit in a tree all day, but now that he was, he really didn't know where to go from there. How do you find a dream? The whole idea seemed ridiculous, really. Because of some vengeful witch, his soul had been taken from him the moment he had become a vampire, and it had joined with his soulmate.

Soulmate. I like the sound of that, he thought, and felt his lips stretch into a wide smile. And because she had his soul, he was connected to her. *I can call her to me ... no, not her, her spirit ...*

Megan? Eric thought the question, feeling a little foolish. *Megan, can you hear me?* He had never really tried to call her before, it had just kind of happened, and he wasn't entirely sure if it would work, even though Mitchell had told him he could do it.

He waited, holding his breath and keeping his eyes glued shut, for what felt like ages. It was then that he realized how quiet she had been over the last hour or so, and his heart twisted and squeezed. He had been so focused on out running his family, who Eric was confident were tracking him, that he hadn't realized that Megan had stopped ...

"Eric? Where am I?" Megan asked, her voice groggy, and then she shrieked, an ear-splitting sound, and Eric's eyes flew open.

Megan straddled the tree branch directly in front of him. Her body was rigid; her white knuckled hands gripped the branch as if her life depended on holding on. Her stunning green eyes were wide with panic, and her beautiful heart was beating like a frenzied drum roll.

"Isn't it obvious," Eric said, and smirked. He reached out, prying her hands from the tree bark, and held them tightly. "You're in a tree, of course."

Megan laughed. It was forced, and it came out in a quick

burst, but the sound sent waves of pleasure over his skin. "How did I get in a tree?" she asked, smiling. "And why is it that every time I close my eyes you magically appear?"

"You're just lucky, I guess." Eric's voice was thick with emotion. *She still thinks I'm a dream.* The thought made his stomach sink. Maybe that was a good thing, he tried to convince himself, but it hurt all the same. He let go of one of her hands and brushed a loose curl from her forehead, letting his fingertips linger on her cheek. Megan blushed, a rosy pink, and a delicate giggle escaped her lips. He wanted to savor the moment, hold onto it, and never let it go. Too bad for him, his mouth didn't feel the same. "Megan, who's chasing you?"

"Excuse me?" Megan asked, looking surprised. She blinked, and lifted a questioning eyebrow.

For a split second, Eric considered telling her everything. About the curse, and the witch, and their entwined souls, but instead, he bit his tongue. She had enough to be scared of; she didn't need to know that she was tied to a vampire—not yet. They could deal with that when he found her. "Who's chasing you?" he asked again, softly, encouragingly.

"How ... how ... how ..." she stammered. She scrunched her forehead and her little button nose, and she narrowed her eyes at him. She let go of his hand and started to cross her arms over her chest, but she teetered and slipped on the branch. Suddenly, her arms flew around his neck for support, and she pulled herself tightly against him.

Eric shook his head, trying not to grin at how adorable she looked right then, and sighed. He gently pushed her back, holding her shoulders tightly, and met her eyes. "I just know, okay?" he said, his tone pleading with her to accept it. "Tell me who and why."

Megan watched him for a long moment, considering something, Eric assumed, although he didn't have the slightest idea as to what. But then she shrugged, just a small lift of her tiny shoulders and sighed. "I don't know who they are. They showed up a few weeks ago when this thing appeared on my neck," she said with distain. She swiped her curls away from her neck and pointed at the soul's mark inked on her skin. "They said it will lead them to a demon. A vampire. But that's impossible. Vampires are not real." She laughed awkwardly, dropping her eyes from his, and her face flushed cherry.

"Yes, impossible." Eric cracked a one sided grin and nodded enthusiastically, hoping that it didn't look fake. The grin felt fake, that was for sure. "If they're waiting for the vampire, then why are they chasing you?" he pressed on, desperate for any piece of information that may help him save her. And he would save her, even if he died trying. Sitting with her, in that tree, right then, felt as if it was the most natural thing, as if it was something that they had done countless times before. It was as if he had always known her, and never known her all at the same time. And the thought of losing her before he actually met her, physically laid eyes upon her, was something that he just could not accept. Not now. Not ever.

"They said if they have to kill me to draw him out they will." Megan sighed then, a long and gusty sound. "I'm losing my mind," she muttered under her breath, before bringing her eyes back to him. "You seem so real ... I've never had dreams like this before." She reached up, entwining her fingers with his, which were still on her shoulders.

"It's quite common to dream up a hero when your life is in danger," Eric said, matter-of-factly, all the while wondering if it was in fact a true statement. He didn't wonder for long though, because she squeezed his hands lightly. Her skin against his felt like silk, and it took every bit of restraint he had not to pull her closer.

"Well, hero, how will you save me then?" she asked teasingly. Her lips quirked upwards, and her eyes danced.

As Eric watched her smile, so carefree and happy in this moment, darkness began to simmer in his belly. It was black as pitch, swirling around him, eating away at him. Someone was trying to take this away from him, and right then he knew that he would kill anyone who tried. She was his. He was as sure of it as he was sure that the grass was green, or the sky, blue. She was the air he breathed; he felt it in his bones and with every beat of his heart.

"Where do you live?" he demanded, a bit too harshly.

Megan gasped, and he heard her pulse quicken. "Eric, what's wrong with your eyes?" she asked, in a barely audible whisper.

"Where do you live!" he yelled. Everything his eyes touched blazed like fire. He tried to pull it back and tamp down the rage that was brewing within him, but he couldn't. It was as if the anger had its own life force, burning within him uncontrollably. His muscles began to tense, shifting under his skin, and she gripped his hands tighter for support as she tried to slide away from him. Looking at her, Eric couldn't tell if she was more afraid of him or of plummeting to the ground from the tree branch they sat on.

"In ... in the mountains," she said, her voice shaking with fear. A trembling hand let go of his and pointed behind him. "But I've been hiding in a cave."

Hiding in a cave! a voice in his mind hissed. That did him in, and he lost the little bit of control he had left. His fangs snapped down, tearing through his gums in a blink.

Megan whimpered, and brought both of her hands to her mouth. Her eyes shimmered with terrified tears. "Oh my God, you ... you ... have fangs." Her voice was muffled, her hands blocking the sound. She tried to move again, sliding backwards towards the thin part of the branch and further away from him. It began to sag and crack, and then it snapped.

Eric reached out a hand to grab her, but he wasn't fast enough. Megan screamed, a bloodcurdling scream, and her arms flapped wildly about her. "I'm coming to find you," he yelled, as she fell. He focused on sending her back, mentally pushing the image of her away, and just before her body hit the ground, she vanished from sight.

CHAPTER 12

That didn't turn out so well, Eric thought miserably, as he looked at the broken tree branch lying below him. Scaring her hadn't really been part of the plan, and it definitely wasn't something she needed right now.

Eric let out a deep sigh. In the back of his mind, he could hear Megan calling him, begging him to come back to her, and for a moment, he thought about doing just that. She whispered apologies. Urging him to believe that she was not scared, even calling him her hero. His heart twisted and thumped erratically. A flash of her neck flitted across his vision. Her soft ivory skin tinted pink as the blood moved underneath the odd marking inked upon her skin. It resembled a figure eight, with a solid line passing through the center of the bottom loop. The outline of it burned brightly, illuminating and glowing in his mind, as if his brain was forcing him to see it. The glow beat in time with her heartbeat, pulsing out towards him. She called to him again. Just his name floating around his head, and then all of a sudden, she was gone. Her scent, her smile, the mark … all of it faded into a small and distant memory.

He shifted his weight on the branch, looking behind him, and as he did, he cringed. Maybe he should have been more specific with his questions. All he could see were rolling mountains stretching out as far as his eyes would reach.

Eric sat there staring, feeling utterly defeated, for a long moment. He was pretty sure that even at top speed it would take him close to a day to reach the bottom of the first mountain. His throat was on fire, he was starving—again— and Megan was in the mountains being hunted because of him. For the first time since the day he had found out what he had become, Eric wished Mitchell had never saved him, and he had died in the field, alone.

****

Starvation was a bitter companion. Since becoming a vampire, Eric had never gone this long without blood, and as the hours passed, his mind began to play tricks on him. With every turn he made, he witnessed Megan's death, each time a more brutal death than the last.

Everything he saw was washed in a permanent crimson haze, and his fangs would not retreat no matter what he tried. But still he pressed forwards.

After his initial desperate defeat, Eric had noticed something. It was small, and he almost missed it, but it was there. A soft pull around his heart, like a wire tightening and humming, pulling him blindly towards the mountains, and the closer he got, and the more frightened Megan became, the stronger it was.

For the first night in weeks, the seemingly endless snow had finally stopped falling. The inky black sky was alive with a blanket of stars, and the moon shone brightly, casting a silver glow upon the snowy ground.

Eric was closing in on the first mountain, the base of it finally coming into sight. He pushed himself a bit harder, trying to run faster. He kept Megan's smile at the forefront of his mind, pushing away all other thoughts. It was her smile that kept him moving. The coy curve of her lips, as if she had a secret that she was inviting him to share—only him. He wondered what she would think when she realized that he was more than just a dream. Would she welcome him? Would she feel the same insistent pull to be near him as he did to her?

Suddenly, the only thing Eric could smell was blood. The sounds of nature were drowned out by a rhythmic pulse, thumping in a slow and even beat, pushing the steaming, mouthwatering liquid through a waiting vein.

His throat burned, and his teeth throbbed. The scent overtook him, clogging his other senses, and robbing him of his restraint. Before he knew it, he zoned in on it, and his course shifted, veering to the right. Something inside him, deep within his belly growled. He needed food. And he needed it now.

As he raced towards the waiting vein, his mind tried to rationalize the persistent hunger that raged through him. Being a vampire had its perks. Immortality, strength, speed, mind control; all of it was a bit unbelievable, and delightfully thrilling. And Eric knew that all of their gifts centered on human blood. Without it, they would not be able to access the power they could wield. And without that power, he would never find her. *Yes,* Eric thought, *I'm hunting for Megan.* He knew the thought was ridiculous, and that hunting was taking him away from his mission, but he couldn't stop.

Eric broke through the trees, and his eyes landed on a tiny whitewashed cottage, nestled in between two towering oaks at the base of the mountain. It was surrounded by a white picket fence, and it almost looked like a dollhouse against the trees.

He stopped, backing up a few steps, and slinked behind the tree line for cover, his eyes scanning for the humans that he could smell.

At first, Eric almost missed them in the dark. But something shifted, something brown, fabric, and his eyes zoned in on them. Three men, all wearing dark cloaks.

Eric snarled; the sound echoed off the mountain. It was

them. The ones chasing her. Adrenaline surged through him like a live wire, and he sprung forwards without thought. He made quick work of the first two, on them and snapping their necks in less than a second. Eric spun to the third one, his face masked by the hood of the cloak, and he stalked towards him.

The man didn't move. He didn't draw the bow that he had dangling in his hand; he didn't even flinch when Eric pounced on him. Eric grabbed the itchy fabric around the man's throat and pushed the hood from his head.

The man locked challenging eyes with Eric, but he did not flinch. "More are here, and more will come," the man said with a throaty chuckle. Eric snarled. All he saw was this man chasing Megan. Whether he had been or not, it didn't matter. Eric bared his fangs and sunk his teeth into the man's neck.

"Eric, stop!" Megan's voice shrieked, rupturing in his ears.

CHAPTER 13

Eric dropped the man abruptly at the sound of Megan's voice and spun around. The man fell at his feet with a thud, groaning softly on the ground.

When Eric spotted Megan, standing less than ten feet away from him, she trembled visibly. She was wearing a long gown of silky white, the bottom blending into the snowy landscape between them. Her heart was erratic, jumping quickly, and then stopping, only to jump again.

"They said that I am marked by the devil," Megan said. "That he has claimed my soul." She rolled her shoulders back, and held her chin high, but she wasn't fooling Eric. Her fear was evident. Her eyes darted around wildly, her fingers fidgeted with the seams of her dress, and the smell of it wafted around her.

Eric chuckled. *The devil.* It sounded about right. Forgetting the man on the ground, he stepped over him, and in a blink, he stood in front of his red haired goddess.

"Are you the devil?" she asked, her voice shaking with small tremors, although she kept her shoulders straight as she tried to hide her fear of him.

I found her! a voice in his head shouted. *I found her.* Eric cocked his head to the side as he gazed into her sad eyes.

She watched him expectantly, waiting, and he grinned. "Do I look like the devil?" His heart was pounding in his throat.

"Yes," she said. She gathered up the bottom of her dress, and tore a strip of fabric from the bottom. Eric watched her curiously, as she gathered the fabric in her hand like a washcloth and began wiping his face. When she was finished, the white fabric was stained scarlet. She gave him a small, shaky smile, dropped the cloth, and then she turned from him and walked to the house. She opened the little picket fence, and without a backwards glance, she marched up the porch steps and vanished inside.

Eric went after the girl who held his soul and heart in the palm of her hand, helpless to do anything else. When he entered the house, warmth washed over him. A welcoming fire flickered in the hearth of the one room cabin, and Megan stood beside it, staring out the window and into the night. She didn't look at him when he entered the room. "I think they will kill me soon," she murmured, as he closed the door.

"Hush now." Eric closed the space between them in four large steps and gathered her in his arms. "Do not speak of such things."

Megan rested her head on his chest, hugging him closely. "I'm not afraid, Eric."

"You are not going to die. I won't let it happen," Eric said with fervor. Now that he had her, he was never letting go. Never. No one would harm her again.

"What can you do? You're only a dream. A figment of my imagination. Something I have conjured up to ease my fears." A small tear glistened as it snaked down her cheek, and she dropped her gaze to the wooden floor. "I'm not naive, Eric. They said I was marked for a devil, so my imagination constructed the devil in my dreams. You are only my mind playing tricks on me, giving me the love that I need before the end and showing me my fears all at once."

"You're sleeping," he breathed, his heart shattering in a burst of sharp-edged pieces. "Megan, you need to tell me where you are," he said desperately, grabbing her chin in his hands and forcing her to meet his eyes.

But she didn't answer. Instead, she rolled up onto the tips of her toes, and kissed him. It was full of longing, rough and deep, and in that moment, Eric was powerless to her touch. All reason left him, everything melted away. It was just them, lost in each other.

It wasn't until morning dawned, and Eric woke up alone, that he realized she had never told him which mountain she was on, or what cave she had crawled into.

****

Eric stood on the lawn outside his house. It looked so daunting, a glaring reminder of his failure. It had been a month, thirty long days, since the last time he had heard Megan's voice or seen her loving eyes and her blood red spiral locks. The vision that had felt so real, now felt like nothing more than a dream.

For the first time in a month, he felt awake—alive. And being alive was mind numbing and empty.

Eric couldn't say how long he stood in front of his house, debating on whether he should enter or leave. Now that he was back, he wasn't so sure that he would be welcomed, or forgiven. Not that he deserved forgiveness. He knew he didn't, not after the way he had treated Mitchell, but a small part of him hoped ...

Eric heaved a sigh and turned his back on the house, ready to leave, when he heard the door creak open. Glancing over his shoulder, he saw Mitchell step out onto the front porch.

"Eric?" Mitchell asked, squinting his eyes against the sunlight.

"Hi, Dad," Eric said with a little—and more than a little awkward—wave.

"Are you leaving?" Mitchell asked, as he jumped down the steps and raced over to him.

Before Eric could so much as offer a word, Mitchell wrapped a firm arm around his shoulder, and started ushering him up the porch steps. "Eric, you look awful," he said. "And you smell horrid."

"Thanks, Dad," Eric said, because he really didn't know what else to say, and Mitchell didn't seem to expect anything else.

He gave Eric's shoulder a squeeze and said, "I'm glad you're home."

Mitchell never asked about Megan, none of them did, and Eric never spoke of her. At first, it was too painful, but then, as time went on, she became a distant memory, feeling more and more like a dream every day. Maybe they were right and someday her spirit would find his again. He knew she was out there, starting a new life. She had to be, because, well, if she wasn't, he wouldn't have a link to humanity, and he did. He felt compassion, and empathy, and he knew it all stemmed from her. And all he could hope was that this life would be kinder to her than the last.

EPILOGUE

Willowberg, 121 years later

Who would have thought that finding green hair dye would be so hard? Eric hadn't. Not that he was complaining. The distraction couldn't have come at a better time.

Today was the day. Mitchell's search was finally coming to an end. After hundreds of years, he had found her. Amelia. It was supposed to be a happy day. But ... for Eric, not so much.

Jealous. That's exactly how Eric felt. Well that and angry. For the last one-hundred and twenty-one years, Eric had somehow managed to slowly let go of Megan, burying the memories deep within him, and now ... now Mitchell had to go and ruin it, resurrecting the love and longing Eric felt for her so long ago.

Mitchell had decided, like this morning, that he was moving out until Amelia settled in, because for some retarded reason that Eric couldn't understand, Mitchell didn't want her to know that they were vampires—yet. But that wasn't even the worst part, not only was he moving out, but he had also given Eric the job of "Amelia's chaperone." Eric had agreed, of course. Really, what choice did he have?

Except, the last thing he needed right now was to surround himself with a lovesick teenage girl.

Eric flipped down the visor and opened up the mirror, inspecting his new hair. The color turned out better than he had thought it would, and it matched his eyes perfectly. *Note to self: next time just go to a hair place first,* Eric thought, realizing how much time he would have saved if he hadn't spent two hours driving around trying to find the right shade (or any shade for that matter) of green. It had been a spur of the moment decision, something to get his mind off Megan, and as he checked himself out, he was glad he did it.

With another quick inspection, he closed the visor and started up his Corvette. The engine purred to life, and he popped the car into gear, pulled away from the curb, and headed towards home.

The drive home took less than ten minutes, and before he knew it, Eric pulled his car up to the gate. He rolled down his window and grinned, when he caught Joe's muffled laughter. "What's so funny?" he asked, innocently glancing at the portly, balding guard in full uniform, except, he was pretty sure Joe was laughing at his hair.

Joe's eyes sparkled with amusement, and he grinned. "The color suits you, Mr. Carter," he said with a chuckle.

"How many times do I have to tell you, call me Eric," he said as sternly as he could, and then he wrinkled his nose. "You make me feel so old."

Joe shrugged, as if to say *get used to it already,* and then he flipped the switch, and the big iron gate clanked open. This had been a daily conversation for years, and still, for some reason, the guard insisted on calling him Mr. Carter. Eric was pretty sure he did it for a laugh, but man, it really *did* make him feel old.

"They here yet?" Eric asked, looking at the road before him.

"Not yet, Mr. Carter." Eric grumbled something, and Joe's smile widened. He rolled up the window, and thrust the car forward through the opened gate, climbing up the hilly street.

When he turned onto the driveway, and the house came into view, he clenched his jaw. It was all arches, turrets, and balconies, with a brown tiled roof and gray stone walls. A present for Amelia. Mitchell had the castle built after one of their dreams. It should have been magical. Seriously, he lived in a bloody castle, but with the way he was feeling, it looked more like a wicked witch's castle than his home.

Eric tried to push the turmoil that was brewing inside him away, because really, he wasn't one of those guys. He liked people. People liked him. Having Amelia around could be ... fun.

He glanced at the clock on his dash. *Twenty minutes. She'll be here in twenty minutes.* Megan's bright eyes surfaced in his mind, and his stomach clenched with anxiety. *Pull it together,* he coached himself. *She's been gone for more than a hundred years.*

With that little pep talk, he maneuvered his Corvette around the west side of the house and into a motor court with large carports on both sides and parked in the empty lot. He hastily turned off the car, jumped out, and then he ran up the stone-covered terrace steps and threw open the French doors leading to the kitchen.

Eric needed to calm his nerves. He padded over to the cherry-wood island. *I need pancakes.* Pancakes made everything better. It was in that moment that he clued in that the driveway had been empty. No one was home. And if no one was home, there was no Mabel to yell at him for cooking.

He set about the kitchen, pulling out a box of pancake mix and a frying pan. After reading the directions, and figuring even he couldn't screw up pancakes, he turned on the stove and added some olive oil to the pan.

Eric carefully measured the mix, added the recommended amount of water, and began to stir, but no matter what utensil he tried, it looked ... lumpy. Was it supposed to look like that? He shifted through the cupboards, looking for something else that might work, and he spotted the blender. *Perfect!* He grabbed it, quickly dumped in the lumpy mix, and plugged the blender in. He was just about to push the button when Mabel walked in, arms loaded with groceries. She dropped them at the door, put her hands on her round hips, and gave him one of her stern *grandmother* looks.

"What are you doing in my kitchen?" she asked, narrowing her eyes further.

Eric grinned. "You weren't here, so I thought I'd make pancakes," he said. The oil in the frying pan began to crackle as it heated.

"With a blender?" she asked, clearly not amused, and she started towards him. She was wearing her favorite flowery apron, and her gray hair was pulled back in a tight bun, making the dirty look she was shooting him appear more severe than it really should have been.

Eric glanced at the blender. *It's a good idea*, he thought. He looked back up at her and grinned, his finger hovering over the button. She was overreacting, he was sure of it. It was just pancakes.

"Eric, no!" she hollered, just as he pushed down, and the blender roared to life.

Okay, maybe, just maybe, Mabel wasn't actually overreacting. As soon as he pushed down, Eric clued in as to why she was yelling. Turns out, blenders have lids, or if they didn't, Eric figured they should. The room exploded in a mess of yellowish pancake batter, coating Eric, and splashing onto Mabel. It dripped from the ceiling and covered the floors. It was a sticky, gooey mess, and Eric laughed.

Well, he laughed until the first strike came. Mabel screamed, a shrill sound that ruptured through him, and then she hit him on the backside with what felt like a stick. He spun around, his foot caught on the cupboard that he had left open, and a bunch of pots and pans clattered to the floor.

"Stop it," he yelled, raising his arms as Mabel swung a broom at him. He jumped back, knocking a glass off the counter, and it crashed to the marble floor, shattering into pieces.

Mabel kept coming at him, screaming unintelligible curses about ruining her kitchen. "Ouch," Eric groaned with amusement, trying to stifle his laughter, which was on the verge of exploding. He raised his arms in an attempt to protect himself from the blows of a broom swishing furiously at him. "It was an accident!" he cried out.

Out of the corner of his eye, he saw Angelle fly through the door, looking furious and right on her heels ... He blinked, and his jaw dropped—literally. *Megan.* Her hair was different, brown, not red, and her eyes ... blue-gray, but everything else was her. Suddenly, she darted over to the fridge and whipped it open, and then Mabel hit him again.

"What the hell is going on?" Angelle yelled, jumping in front of Mabel. She snatched the broom and tossed it. It flew across the room, and slammed into the wall before clattering to the marble floor. "That's enough." She turned to Eric, grabbing him by the shoulder, and shoved him away, hard. Hard enough that his shoulder popped out of its joint and he had to bite back a growl as he snapped it back into place.

It's not her. It's not her. It's not her. She's Mitchell's. Amelia. But even if he knew it ... *dammit!* How was he going to survive this? Eric watched the girl run over to the stove, and that's when he noticed the fire. She dumped a box of something on the burning grease-lit frying pan. The fire extinguished in a billowing cloud of smoke, and she started to cough.

"He's ruining my kitchen. Look at this mess!" Mabel cried in a tizzy, surveying the mess.

Eric was rubbing his shoulders, looking at Angelle, because he seriously couldn't look at the girl any longer. "I was just trying to make pancakes for Amelia," he said. The name felt wrong on his tongue; he thought that the little lie might smooth over the mess, and then, because he couldn't seem to keep his eyes off of her, he gave the girl a bashful smile. Then he looked back over at Angelle and said, "And in case you missed it, she was hitting me. Why did you shove me like that?"

Angelle rolled her eyes in a dramatic show of annoyance. "I'm sure you deserved it, Eric. You usually do." She looked over at Mabel, who was now scurrying around the kitchen, trying to clean up the mess. "What did he do, Mabel?"

"He used a blender without the lid," Mabel said. Her voice was stern and a touch motherly. And she looked absolutely fit to be tied.

Eric shrugged. "Stirring was taking too long." His heart was jumping into his throat, and he could barely catch his breath. He snuck a peek at the girl, and it took everything he had not to run to her and take her in his arms.

"You're such a dork—and what's with the hair?" Angelle laughed, pulling him out of his thoughts. "You look like a little punk."

"Don't knock the hair," Eric said, leaning back against the island, arms folded across his chest.

"You can't go to the office like that," Angelle said.

"Don't have to. I've been promoted to personal chauffeur. And I think it looks great. I thought you would appreciate it." He batted his eyes and struck a pose. "It totally matches my eyes." He looked Amelia over again, and then pushed off from the counter, strolling towards her, and he felt a grin spread across his face. He dropped into a gallant bow, and a cute little giggle slipped from her lips. He took her hand in his, and kissed it lightly. "Welcome, my lady," he said playfully.

Angelle groaned. "You are such a moron."

Eric forced a laugh and dropped Amelia's hand. If he had hoped that his skin would sizzle as it did when he had touched his Megan, he was disappointed. He strolled back over to the island, and leaned lazily, elbows propping him up.

"This is Mabel," Angelle said with laughter in her voice. "She's our housekeeper, cook, and den mother."

"Hello, dear. How was your trip?" Mabel asked distractedly.

"It was okay," Amelia answered, with the same sweet tones that Megan's voice held. As she spoke, he watched her intently, waiting, wishing she would show some sign, any sign, that she felt something, anything, being so close to him.

"That's good, dear. Look at this disaster." Mabel let out a long, exasperated sigh. "At least I caught him before he burnt the house down." She paused, scrubbing at the counters. "Why in the world were you making pancakes? It's almost dinner time."

"She had a long trip," he shrugged. "Thought she'd be hungry." Eric was still leaning against the counter, watching the girl, scanning her over from head to toe. Her heart was racing, fluttering like a humming bird's wings, and it was the most beautiful sound he had ever heard.

"We just finished rebuilding the kitchen from the last time Eric tried to cook," Angelle added.

"Um, can I help clean up?" Amelia asked, and took a small step towards the sink, looking around.

"That's okay, dear," Mabel said. "You two run along now, and I'll clean up this mess." Mabel made a shoo-ing gesture and shot Eric a look, not a good one.

"That's her nice way of saying get out of my space," Angelle said, ushering the girl away from the mess. "Believe me, you don't want to stay and help. Come on, I'll give you the grand tour." Angelle snagged the girl's hand and started pulling her through the kitchen. As they went, Angelle glanced over her shoulder at him and said, "Eric, bring Millie's bag to her room."

"Make the tour quick," Mabel said. "I don't want you to be late for dinner. I'm making your favorite, Amelia, Fettuccini Alfredo with chicken."

Angelle towed her through an open doorway, out of the kitchen, and into the living room.

The girl snuck a peek over her shoulder at Eric, catching him staring. His eyes met hers, and his heart stopped. They drew him in, and everything around him vanished. She flushed, and her beautiful heart fluttered. He had an overwhelming urge to run to her, pull her in his arms, and sink his teeth into her neck. He wanted to claim her. He wanted his name to appear on her neck. She licked her lips, and right then he knew he could, and she would let him.

She's not yours! his conscious hissed, breaking the spell. He blinked and gave his head a little shake. She gasped, and he forced a grin on his face. He winked at her and turned away, leaving the kitchen as fast as he could.

Crap! Crap! Crap! The word echoed through his brain with each step he took. How the hell could this happen? What if Mitchell was wrong? Okay, Eric knew that was impossible. You can't be wrong about the soulmate bond. It just doesn't happen. Mitchell had been dreaming about that ... that ... girl for five years. *But ... but ...* his brain couldn't finish the thought.

Eric rushed into his bedroom, closing the door, and leaned against it. He didn't know how he would survive this or even if he could. No matter what his brain told him, his heart was pulling him in another direction. And his stupid, reckless heart was sure that his father's Amelia was, in fact, his Megan.

ABOUT THE AUTHOR

Ashley Stoyanoff is an author of paranormal romance books for young adults, including The Soul's Mark series and the Deadly Trilogy. She lives in Southern Ontario with her husband, Jordan, and two cats: Tanzy and Trinity.

In July 2012, Ashley published her first novel, The Soul's Mark: FOUND, and shortly thereafter, she was honored with The Royal Dragonfly Book Award for both young adult and newbie fiction categories.

An avid reader, Ashley enjoys anything with a bit of romance and a paranormal twist. When she's not writing or devouring her latest read, she can be found spending time with her family, watching cheesy chick flicks or buying far too many clothes.

Ashley loves hearing from her readers, so feel free to connect with her online.

www.ashleystoyanoff.com
www.facebook.com/AshleyStoyanoffTheSoulsMark
www.goodreads.com/ashley_stoyanoff

Read on for a preview of The Soul's Mark: HUNTED, Book 2 of The Soul's Mark series.

CHAPTER 1

The wind whipped through Amelia's hair as the door opened. She felt alive; pure adrenaline pumped through her body. It was a dizzying and exciting kind of rush. One she had never experienced before.

Mitchell's hands grasped her shoulders so tightly that she winced. He whimpered, and she was pretty sure she heard a shriek, a sound that she had never before heard from him. She glanced over her shoulder and reached up to squeeze his hand. She couldn't stop the burst of laughter that erupted from her belly.

The sounds of her laughter were drowned out by the rumbling engines of the plane and the windstorm that blustered around them, and she wondered how on earth she had heard his shriek. Then she noticed his slightly pink cheeks and the emanating feelings of embarrassment, and she realized she was feeling it through the bond.

You've got to be kidding me? she sent through her sidesplitting laughter, as she took in his ghostly complexion. *You're scared?*

We're really, um, high, Mitchell whimpered into her mind. He sounded like a scared little child, and he took a few steps back, pressing his body firmly against the wall. *I don't think I can do this. What if my parachute doesn't open?*

Oh, honey, Amelia said, crossing the short distance

between them and caressing his pale cheeks. She smirked, dropping her thoughts to a gentle whisper. *You know you're a vampire, right? Even if it doesn't open, you'll be fine.*

She felt Mitchell groan. *You really aren't helping, love.*

Suddenly the plane hit a bit of turbulence, jostling them around, and he screeched, an ear piercing, little girl kind of sound. He pulled her into his arms, holding onto her so tightly, as if she was the only thing that could save him—his stable rock.

She squeezed him back just as firmly, feeling the fear tremble through his muscles and the panic that he pushed into her mind. She stood up on tiptoes and kissed the tip of his nose. *Now, this is new,* she pushed the thought to him. *I think I could get used to being the strong one.*

He chuckled, or at least that was what Amelia thought he was trying to do. It sounded more like a gurgling sob. He rubbed his nose, side to side against hers. *In case...In case...* He shook his head, as if he couldn't bear to finish the words. His lips twitched up into an unconvincing smile. *I love you.*

Amelia almost laughed again. Who would have thought that Mitchell, of all people, would be scared of heights? Or scared of anything for that matter. But before the giggles could explode, he silenced them with a hungry kiss. His lips worked over hers with such an urgency and fierceness that Amelia was quickly swept away, forgetting the plane, forgetting the wind, forgetting everything around them. It was just them. Together. Nothing else in the world mattered. Not a single other thing existed apart from him.

"If you're going to jump, you've got to do it now," the coach shouted, ruining the moment.

Reluctantly, Amelia pulled her lips away, panting. She locked eyes with Mitchell. "We don't have to do this," she yelled, although it floated through the air like a hushed whisper, thanks to the almost deafening wind blowing around them, and she tried to hide the disappointment in her voice.

His gaze shifted quickly to the open doorway, and then

back to her. He took a shaky breath, cupped her face with his soft and clammy hands, and a scared thought trembled into her mind, *Can you push me out?*

Amelia grinned and nodded in response. Her heart swelled and jumped around in her chest. How had she gotten so lucky? How many other men would jump out of a plane, just because their girlfriend wanted to?

"Guys, you really have to jump, like now," the coach shouted again.

Mitchell visibly shivered. *What if I land on a twig and it pierces my heart?* He sent the thought through their bond, and she could tell he didn't trust his voice.

I've got it covered, honey, Amelia sent back, coating the thoughts with a soothing tone.

How? he breathed.

Amelia leaned into him, stretching up and brushing her lips against his ear, as if she was going to whisper a secret. But even this close and with his enhanced hearing, she knew she would have to yell to be heard over the noise. *We're going to land in the lake. That's why he's rushing us.*

Mitchell looked more horrified than reassured. *But what if we get tangled in the ropes, what if our parachutes drag us underwater, what if...*

Amelia cut off Mitchell's rambling thoughts and again reassured him, *Shhh...We'll be fine.*

It had taken some arranging, but using her magic to pull on Mitchell's power of persuasion, she had managed to arrange for them to jump alone, over a lake. They wouldn't have an instructor, and they didn't have to be secured together, although, she planned to use a little magic to keep them together as they fell through the sky.

He took her hand, lacing their fingers together, and inched towards the opening. *Don't let go?* he said, as if it was a question.

Never, Amelia answered, and she meant it. Never again would she let him slip away. They locked gazes, and together, they jumped.

Amelia was the first to scream as they tumbled, but it wasn't from fear. *Mitch, you're going to break my hand,* she sent in a panicked rush.

He loosened his grip to a bearable tension and sent a blast of shame through the bond. *I didn't want you to know I'm such a wuss,* he sent.

With her free hand, she pulled him closer to her, lacing their hands together with steamy golden strands of power that wrestled against the wind that tried to rip them apart. *You're not a wuss,* she pushed the thought to him. *You're the strongest person I know, and I love you, Mitchell Lang.*

He gave her a genuine smile, and for just a second, the fear vanished from his eyes. Bright, warm sunshine poured through the bond. Amelia soaked it up, basking in his love. The emotions wrapped around her, seeped into her skin, and filled her soul. Mitchell leaned closer and kissed her with just a light peck, and then he cleared his throat and yelled, "Can we pull the cord?" The fear crept back onto his face.

She reached to her side and he mimicked her movements, clasping the cord tightly, and together, they pulled. As the parachutes opened, the wind caught them and they jerked up. Mitchell screeched and Amelia grinned, keeping a tight hold on his hand. It took a moment for the ballooning chutes to fill out, but when they did, it was amazing. Floating down over the crystal clear lake, the world around them was breathtaking. A sight that Amelia was sure was now etched into her mind. The glistening water, the rolling hills, the little cottage. From above, it was just all the more beautiful. She lost herself, allowing the vastness of the earth below to fill her soul and the closeness of Mitchell to warm her heart.

This past week had been wonderful, and floating from the sky seemed like the perfect way to end their perfect vacation. Amelia had been a little apprehensive when Mitchell had suggested that they go away—just the two of them. To her pleasant surprise, without all the stress of running a town full of vampires and dealing with an amazing, yet demanding family, they actually had a great time. She would have sworn it wasn't possible, but this time with him had brought them back to the dreams. Back to the times when all that mattered was each other.

The time alone had been full of firsts: their first real date—*alone*; the first time to the movies; he even bought her flowers for the first time. It had been more than she could have ever imagined. And for the first time since they had met, she actually felt like they were just a normal couple, having a normal life, and best of all, she realized how much she truly loved him. The way he smiled at her, the way he caressed her cheek. How his eyes sparkled when he laughed, and the way he always opened the door for her. She loved him. Everything about him. *Would it be like this when they got back?* she wondered, as the ground approached. Mitchell tightened his grip on her hand, pulling her from her musing.

Amelia squeezed back, trying to reassure him, and then she focused on the fall. She gathered up her magic, pulling the energy together and letting the golden strands wrap around both of them. Their momentum slowed, and she felt like a feather drifting in the wind as they descended the last few feet. When they landed, the cool lake water gently splashed up around them.

"Mitch, you can open your eyes," Amelia said, as the parachutes billowed around them, landing in the hip-deep water.

"Is it over?" he asked, keeping his eyes squeezed tightly shut.

Amelia laughed. "Okay, now you're acting like a wuss." She gave him a playful nudge and then unclipped the chutes. She was about to start wading in towards the beach, when suddenly his lips were on hers, in a hard, breathtaking kiss.

"I can't believe we actually did that," he said when they finally came up for air. And then a grin spread across his lips, and he scooped her up in his arms. Amelia gawked at him in amazement as he carried her out of the water. She had never seen him so happy before. So content. And seeing him like this made her happier than she had ever been before.

Mitchell was still grinning as he set her down on the beach, and she smiled up at him. "I'm the luckiest girl in the world," she said, and then giggled at the amount of emotion that came out in her words. "I love you."

"I love you, too," Mitchell said, leaning down, pressing his warm lips to hers. And in that moment, everything melted away. The sounds of the chirping birds and the soft crashing waves were gone. All that was left was him. And he was all hers.

CHAPTER 2

Looking back, Amelia figured she should have known that the *honeymoon phase* wouldn't last. She had really wanted to believe that maybe, just maybe, the vacation had worked. Perhaps the magical perfection they resurrected while they were away would remain, and it did–sort of. They hadn't fought for about three weeks, but realistically, long-term bliss didn't seem entirely possible now. Something was definitely different, something seemed wrong, and no matter how hard she tried, Amelia just couldn't put her finger on it.

They fought. That's just what they did. It wasn't something to be proud of by any means; she hated to admit it, but their squabbles made them work, and she kind of, sort of, missed it. She had always believed that fighting was healthy to a certain extent. Yell a little, say what's on your mind, and with it out in the open, it's easier to get over the issue and move on. But since they had returned, Mitchell had been distant, on edge, and overly sensitive.

For a quick second, Amelia thought about sneaking a peek into his mind. What was the point of having a link to each other's thoughts if they weren't going to use it? Besides, she was dying to know where he had taken off to in such a rush. Her brain tried to reason with her, insisting that one little peek wouldn't hurt. A little bit of information now could prevent a slew of misunderstandings later. That's a good thing, right? But her heart couldn't do it; it pleaded and begged her not to snoop. It twisted and turned, insisting that she let things be.

Part of their agreement eight months ago was to stay out of each other's minds. It had been Amelia's idea, and she had been adamant that their bond should only be used for emergencies—no more snooping. And no matter what, no matter how much she was itching to snoop, she wasn't going to be the first to break that rule, even if it was torture not knowing whatever it was that she didn't know.

They had been about to go for a swim when his cell phone rang, and to her disbelief, Mitchell—strong, in control Mitchell—actually jumped when it started to ring. He tried to hide his anxiety from her, but thanks to the bond (or maybe cursed by the bond; Amelia wasn't sure) she felt every bit of turmoil that bounced around in him during that very short call. After a few *yes's,* Mitchell hung up, and then without any real explanation, only saying he had some business to attend to, he had taken off. She knew, just knew, he was hiding something—something big—and her suspicion was driving her crazy.

Amelia huffed, and instead of checking in, she threw a tank top and a pair of shorts on over her bikini and then stomped out of her bedroom and onto the terrace, gazing over the vast gardens while deep in thought. Had she made the right decision? She wasn't sure, and she couldn't help but wonder if putting a limit on their connection was actually the right thing to do. Amelia knew she should think of it as a gift. Most people would kill to know the inner workings of their boyfriend's mind. Even so, Amelia knew all too well that knowing everything wasn't always a good thing. It led to anger, jealousy and, above all else, danger for their friends.

It was an unseasonably warm night for mid-April. Amelia glanced at the thermometer and wasn't surprised that it was still 90 degrees. In spite of only wearing lightweight clothes, she felt sticky and gross from the humidity. There wasn't even a touch of a breeze to ease the discomforting heat.

The sky was alive with heat lightning that danced through the clouds, and the far off rumble of thunder signaled the approaching rain. Amelia hopped down the steps and strolled over to the pear-shaped pool. The water looked so alluring and almost magical with streaks of silver as the lighting continued its rain dance. A few scattered droplets of rain fell around her, light and refreshing. She perched at the edge of the pool and dipped her feet in the cool water.

Amelia guessed she should have been happy. Over the last few months, she had really made some headway with Mitchell. With some careful planning and a touch of flirty manipulation, she was able to convince him to put a stop to the hunting and lift the curfew in their little gated community.

But really, stopping the hunting was a must. Amelia remembered when she had first arrived in Willowberg and found out her little gated community was actually a hunting ground for vampires. The thought of it still turned her stomach. Really, it was the twenty-first century. They can't just go around killing people like barbaric cavemen.

It had taken months of arguing, but in the end, she had convinced Mitchell to put a stop to it. And with that *win*, he had slowly started to back off, treating her like an equal and not like a precious little flower that always needed protection. But lately, there had been a shift in the incredible balance they had found. Instead of dictating what she could and couldn't do, he was using sugar to get his way. And that was really, really infuriating. Especially since Amelia was positive that he was using this oversensitive, sugary attitude to get his own way. How could you say no to someone who was just so damn sweet?

"Millie, what are you doing out here?" Eric called, ripping her from her thoughts. Not that she minded. In truth, she was relieved not to be alone with her thoughts.

They could be dangerous—destructive. "Where's Mitch?"

Amelia glanced over at him, and her breath caught in her throat. Eric was shirtless and looking incredibly yummy in his snug cut-off jeans. He wandered towards her, and she couldn't help but admire his perfectly sculpted six-foot frame. He was grinning at her with a grin that Amelia was sure had broken many hearts and turned even more girls into giggling fools. Despite her best efforts, she was not immune to his charm. His leafy-green hair was dripping wet, and the drops beaded on his chest. His vibrant green eyes twinkled with mischief.

Eric plopped down beside her and sprawled out on the dampened lawn, stirring up the sweet scent of fresh-cut grass. His grin spread even wider, and he chuckled. "Better not stare at me like that, Millie. Mitch could be watching." He said it jokingly, but there was something in his voice that sounded strained, and Amelia was sure there was a hint of longing that she forced herself to ignore.

Things weren't easy between them. Not since their little kiss. The kiss still lingered in her mind, popping up occasionally. His sweet and soft, moist lips. His musky scent. *Stop it!* Amelia scolded herself silently. For the life of her, she couldn't understand why the memory was still so vivid. From what she had read and been told about the soulmate bond, she knew she shouldn't even be able think about anyone other than Mitch, especially since he had bitten her, strengthening their link and claiming her as his mate. But there was just something about Eric that made her tingle all over.

Amelia swallowed hard and tried to tell herself it was okay to admire, because Eric was so oh-my-God hot, and she would have to be a complete freak not to notice. As long as it didn't go any further than that, it was fine, right? She gave herself a shake and then grinned at him. "Didn't you have a date?"

Eric's gentle gaze turned into a fierce glare. "Don't change the subject. Where's Mitch?"

Amelia tried to glare back at him, but it was useless. Eric always seemed to know when something was up with her, and it was hard to resist opening up to him. He was exactly that kind of guy. The kind of guy you just wanted to spill all your secrets to. "Don't know. He just took off," she huffed, annoyed that she sounded so whiny.

"What?" He looked genuinely surprised; his eyebrows lifted so high that it looked as if they were about to jump right off his face. "You and Mitch have been getting along great since you got back from the lake. He even moved into your room. What's up?"

"I don't know, Eric," Amelia snapped and shifted her gaze back to the water. She swished her feet violently, sending out waves of ripples. The water sloshed up her legs, leaving puddles all the way up to her thighs. "And he may have moved into my room, but he set up a cot. He won't touch me," she said, glancing at him with a quick look. She felt a hot and rosy blush creeping all the way up her neck, settling onto her cheeks. She wasn't sure why she had told him, but man it felt good to get rid of some of her frustration.

The good feeling vanished far too fast. Eric laughed and then coughed over it, trying to cover it up. "Damn girl, you're kidding me, right?"

Amelia bristled. "Seriously, Eric, I don't want to talk about my lack of a sex life with you. I don't know why I even said it."

He tossed up his hands in surrender, and the laughter vanished. "Whoa, sorry I asked."

Amelia flopped back onto the grass, keeping her feet in the water and groaned. "What about you? You had that hot date tonight."

"Yeah, I canceled it."

Amelia tilted her head towards him and raised a questioning brow. "Why?"

They locked eyes for an uncomfortable minute, and Amelia wished she understood the feelings she had for him.

It was a jumbled mess of emotions—not a single one made any sense. She wondered if she had met Mitchell first, if he had been the one to greet her, would she even notice Eric now. *Probably.* There was just something between her and Eric. A fierce spark. And the weirdest part about it was that every now and then, she felt as strongly for Eric as she did for Mitchell—as if she was bonded to both.

But Amelia knew that was impossible. There was no such thing as two soulmates. Although at one point, Amelia could have sworn that there was no such thing as soulmates at all. She would have been happy to believe that they were just a foolish romantic idea. Maybe it was her stupid witch powers that were interfering. Or maybe she still had doubts about Mitchell. Maybe? Who was she trying to kid? Hell yes, she doubted Mitchell, doubted their bond, doubted everything about their relationship.

When it had been just her and Mitchell, alone in the middle of nowhere, life had been beyond perfect. No distractions, no business, nothing but time to get to know each other. But now, back in the real world with real problems, it was just...

Just when Amelia thought the look would never end, Eric whispered, "I've been dreaming."

Amelia let his words bounce around her brain. If he meant what she thought he meant, then why did he look so defeated? Shouldn't he be ecstatic? He definitely did not look pleased. She tossed around a bunch of different things to say. She wanted to be happy for him. She really did, but he looked just so upset, so broken. She swallowed hard, plastered on a smile, and said, "That's awe..."

The words fell short. Amelia was abruptly cut off by a girl screeching, "Help me!" In a flash, Amelia and Eric both jumped to their feet. Eric took off towards the tree line with vampire-speed before Amelia even figured out where the screaming was coming from.

"Help!" another cry sounded.

Amelia started running in the direction of the cries. Eric

had already disappeared through the willows at the back of the property, and she broke through the trees at a breakneck run, colliding with Eric. He gave her a sideways look, eyes washed with crimson and fangs down. "Go," he snarled.

Amelia flinched, and she really had to fight not to run. If there was one thing she had learned over the last eight months, it was to not show fear. The vampires could smell it, and they thrived on it. Even the friendliest of them could lose control and mistake a friend for a tasty snack when the hunting instincts kicked in.

Eyes still fixed on Amelia, he growled, "Fiona," in a lethal undertone. "Put her down. There's no hunting here."

Fiona? The hair on the back of Amelia's neck rose, and a prickling chill rushed down her spine. She pushed past Eric and froze mid step. Her eyes settled on Fiona.

In theory, Amelia understood the concept of feeding. It wasn't as if she had never been bitten before. With Mitchell, the bite was tender, pleasurable, filled with intense emotions. It brought them together, connecting them on a whole new level. It was almost as if, in those blissful moments, they were one. One person, one soul; they were whole.

However, what Amelia now saw before her was nothing like she experienced with Mitchell. Fiona looked like a prostitute gone mad, clutching a young girl in her arms. Her normally runway model perfect hair was a wild mess. The tangled black strands fell into her blazing eyes, making her pallid complexion look unearthly and almost colorless. She snarled at Amelia, flashing razor sharp fangs, and a trickle of blood dripped down her chin and stained her lacy, orange tank top. Her black spandex shorts left little to the imagination. They were so tiny that they looked more like a pair of boy-cut underwear than shorts, and she was wearing a pair of coal-black knee-high leather boots.

The girl was crying so hard that her screams were scarcely heard, coming out instead as strangled coughs. Fiona held her by the wrist effortlessly as she struggled to get away. Amelia drew in a steadying breath, hoping to come off as unruffled. She wasn't sure if she could pull it off. In truth, she was shaking like a rattlesnake's tail on the inside. She squared her shoulders and focused all her attention on Fiona. "Let her go," she said with a ringing authority that she didn't even know she had in her.

Fiona threw her head back, her long jet-black hair fanning wildly around her face, and her laugh was pure evil. "Oh, Millie, I thought I told you before. You're nothing; Mitch is the one who rules, not you." Fiona gave a big toothy smile, and her gold nugget eyes streaked red. "Besides, he's the one that gave me permission to hunt here. If you have an issue with this, you should take it up with him."

Amelia opened her mouth and then closed it, completely stunned. Had Fiona just said what she thought she said? Mitchell gave her *permission*? The idea was ludicrous. Or was it?

Right then, Eric made a move towards Fiona and everything after that happened in a blurry mess. Fiona sunk her teeth into the girl's neck. The girl screamed a terrifyingly, agonizing sound. White-hot rage surged through Amelia, and she bellowed through the bond, *Mitchell!*

That was all it took for him to tune in, and she instantly felt the hum of him sifting through her thoughts, picking out her location, her surroundings, and looking for any danger. When he put all the pieces together, a mix of panic and rage flooded in so fast she staggered back.

Get away from them, Amelia! Mitchell shouted, the thoughts erupting inside her mind as loud as the booming thunder above.

Eric wrestled Fiona off the girl, and she collapsed in a bloody mess. Amelia dropped down beside her and pushed herself into action, quickly checking for a pulse. When she finally found the faint heartbeat, she let out a pent-up breath.

"Eric," she hollered. "Eric, help me!" She frantically ripped off her top, balled it up, and pressed it against the girl's neck, trying to stop the steady stream of blood. She had never seen anyone bleed so much from a bite, and she was sure Fiona must have hit an artery.

Amelia wanted to scream. The girl couldn't be more than twenty-one years old. She was dirty and ragged looking, as if she hadn't been home in months, maybe years. Her jeans were torn, her hair was a knotted, blondish-gray mess, and Amelia couldn't even begin to make out what color her shirt had been through the layers upon layers of dirt and grime.

Mitchell's panicked yells ruptured through their bond in a tidal wave of fear, but to Amelia, it was just a buzz of noises as she tried to stop the bleeding. How could he permit hunting? And Fiona. Did he really know Fiona was back? He had sworn to her that it would stop—it had stopped. No one was allowed to hunt, not here, not in Willowberg.

The blood was soaking right through her top, and no matter how hard Amelia pressed, she couldn't make it stop. She was talking to the girl; she was vaguely aware that her lips were moving, but she didn't know what she was saying. It sounded mumbled, distorted, and nothing like her own voice. Suddenly, the girl's eyes flew open, and a small tear slid down her cheek. "I'm cold," she whispered.

Amelia stared down at her, incapable of speaking, unable to move. The blood. So much blood. The last time she has seen that much blood, gushing like the rapids of a river, was when her parents died.

Suddenly, Mitchell was there, pulling her away and into his arms. "No!" Amelia screamed. "Let go!" She pulled and struggled, trying to get out of his grasp. "I have to help her," she pleaded, as she thrashed about in his arms. "We have to save her."

"She's gone, Amelia," Mitchell whispered, caressing her hair and holding her tightly to his chest.

"No!" Amelia cried, looking up at him. "She's breathing. Do something! Change her. Please don't let her die." She watched a montage of expressions cross his brow—contemplation, guilt, pain, anger, before finally settling into a cold and closed remoteness.

"I'll do it," Eric offered. He shot a menacing look at Fiona that clearly said, *Don't move,* and then he took a step towards the girl. Her breath was ragged, coming out in short, shallow bursts, and her eyes were wide with fear.

"No, you will not," Mitchell ordered, and as if the storm was helping him to make a point, a bolt of lightning streaked through the sky, illuminating his strong jaw, which was set in a rigid line. He waited for the rumbling thunder to diminish before he said, "She will not be changed."

A wave of blistering heat hit Amelia hard and fury engulfed her from his cruel and heartless words. She let her magic push through her body, gathering it in the pit of her stomach. She let it simmer there, warming her blood and swirling around, and waited for it to boil into a burning ball of lava. When she felt as if she would burst into flames at any moment, she let it loose. "You are a bastard!" she screamed. "Let go of me."

Stripes of gold, like rays from the sun, shot from every inch of her skin, and Mitchell snarled as the steamy energy hit him, tossing him back. Fiona gasped and her already pale skin turned ghostly, but Amelia didn't care who she scared. She let her anger consume her. The swirling storm in her belly was kicked up a notch as Mitchell's rage began to mix with her own. Without thinking, she pulled on it, twisting it into a fiery ball of wrath, letting his emotions fuel another blast of magic, which she launched at him. With an excruciating howl, he crumpled to his knees.

"Ahem, err…Millie," Eric said in an excessively cautious voice. "Um, can you rein it in a little?" He took a few unsure steps closer to her and placed himself in front of Mitchell. "Come on, sweetie. You can control this." He cupped her face gently and gave her an encouraging look.

Amelia, please, Mitchell's terrified voice filled her mind, and as if he had flipped a switch, the sound of his voice— deep and velvety— brought her back to the here and now, and the golden ribbons of magic pulled back and flaked away.

Her knees trembled from exertion, and she drew in a winded breath. She slumped to the ground and put pressure back on the girl's neck. The bleeding was slowing, but there was so much blood on the ground that Amelia wasn't sure if it would help any. When she could find her voice, she glanced back at Eric and pleaded, "Please save her."

Before her eyes could process the movement, Mitchell had rolled up to his feet and grabbed Eric by the arm. "Eric, you will not change her."

Eric let his head drop, refusing to look at Amelia, and she knew she had lost. He wouldn't help her either. "Sorry. I just…"

"Fiona," Mitchell growled, cutting Eric off. "Don't even think about moving."

Amelia stared up at Mitchell blankly, not comprehending. All she could think was, *she's so young.* A small whimper filled her ears, and then Amelia looked back at the girl. She met Amelia's eyes; a stream of blood ran from her neck, and she choked on the air as she tried to suck in a breath. Her lips twitched up, into a dreamlike kind of smile, and then her eyes slowly went vacant.

Amelia sat back on her heels and tightened her arms around her chest in a hug. The warning signs were all there. This was all her fault—she just knew it. She knew Mitchell was hiding something from her. She knew there was something wrong. Why hadn't she figured it out? She was supposed to be the smart one. How? Why? The questions were flying around so quickly that she couldn't seem to grasp onto one. The only thing she was certain of was, without a doubt, this was her fault. She let her guard down and now…

Amelia, you don't understand, Mitchell sent silently and

squeezed her shoulder.

"Don't," she said, quickly getting up from the ground and taking a step back, refusing to use their link to reply to him, not wanting to let him in or feel close to him. She shrugged away his touch. A blissful hush fell over her, and warmth rushed through her body in waves. It took everything she had to bury the uncontrollable urge to fling herself into his arms. To her dismay, no matter how much she wanted to scream at him, she couldn't stop her stupid heart from fluttering erratically as he pushed the feelings to her, trying to calm her and wipe away the horror she had just witnessed. She sucked in a deep breath and let the feelings steady her. Then she said, "Eric, go get Ty and tell him what happened here. Tell him to make arrangements."

"No, I'll handle it," Mitchell said. He reached out to touch her again, and she flinched away. For a brief second, she was sure she saw an inkling of hurt pass across his eyes, but it was so quick, that even with the bond, she wasn't entirely sure.

"Are you going to handle the mess this will cause in the human community?" she retorted, bitterly.

As if he was flicking through the television channels, Mitchell's demeanor abruptly changed from a warm and cozy fire to a winter ice storm. The cold icicle-like stare he gave her sent a rolling chill over her shoulders. "Like I said, you don't understand. Leave Tyler out of this and go wait for me at the house." He groped in his pocket and fished out his cell phone.

Stunned, Amelia put her hands on her hips, opened her mouth, closed it, gathered her thoughts, and then said, "You can't just cover this up, Mitch. And don't order me around. I'm not one of your little followers."

"Amelia," he snapped. And then he went on, keeping his words between them. *Go! I cannot deal with your drama right now.* He glared at her, long and hard, and then fixed his cool stare on Eric. "Take Fiona to my office and wait for me."

www.ingramcontent.com/pod-product-compliance
Lightning Source LLC
Chambersburg PA
CBHW030605130626
46552CB00006B/2663